The roar was terrible now.

Amy's heart banged against her ribs. Another wall of water! How could it be happening?

Amy grasped the rope with one hand, Rick with the other, and pushed into the cliff with all her might. Instantly the area filled with churning floodwaters.

Amy gasped as a red tongue swept away their fire. She screamed when a chunk of land broke off, toppling Rick's pack and forcing him to leap away.

Everything gone and now us! Seconds more and the water was over their feet.

"Riveting...Ruckman's [portrayal of] nature at its most beautiful and most vicious will draw readers onward." —ALA *Booklist*

"Taut, thoughtful and exciting adventure." —*The Kirkus Reviews*

NO WAY OUT

Ivy Ruckman

A Harper Keypoint Book

Library of Congress Cataloging-in-Publication Data
Ruckman, Ivy.
    No way out.

    Summary: Hiking along the Virgin River
in Utah, nineteen-year-old Amy, her brother,
and five friends battle a flash flood.
    [1. Floods—Fiction. 2. Survival—Fiction.
3. Hiking—Fiction. 4. Utah—Fiction] I. Title.
PZ7.R844No 1988   [Fic]   87-47817
ISBN 0-690-04669-3
ISBN 0-690-04671-5 (lib. bdg.)

(A Harper Keypoint book)
ISBN 0-06-447003-2 (pbk.)

Published in hardcover by Thomas Y. Crowell, New York.
First Harper Keypoint edition, 1989.
Harper Keypoint books are published
by Harper & Row, Publishers, Inc.

This one is for my friends.

A ground party scouring the Zion Narrows for the missing hikers was forced by heavy thunderstorms to turn back again on Monday.

The search resumed Tuesday under clear skies when parents rented a plane and flew over the Narrows. "The pilot of the plane reported negative results," Park officials said.

According to longtime residents of the area, the rains Sunday morning were the heaviest in more than a quarter of a century.

—News Release

The Zion Narrows

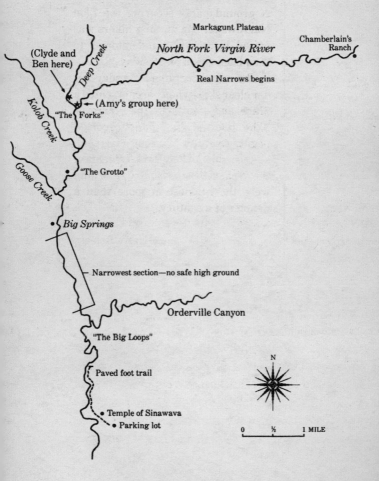

Markagunt Plateau

North Fork Virgin River

Chamberlain's Ranch

Deep Creek

(Clyde and Ben here)

Real Narrows begins

Kolob Creek

← (Amy's group here)

"The Forks"

Goose Creek

"The Grotto"

Big Springs

Narrowest section—no safe high ground

Orderville Canyon

"The Big Loops"

Paved foot trail

Temple of Sinawava

Parking lot

N

0   ½   1 MILE

NO WAY OUT

1

M&M's . . . an orange . . . a swig from the water bottle . . . ten whole minutes to rest in the shade of a stream cottonwood . . .

Amy pressed her cheek against the stickery desert grass and smiled. How had they managed to pull it off—the ultimate hike and a gorgeous hot Saturday to go with it? She and Rick had been looking forward to doing the Zion Narrows all summer. Now, lying facedown on her folded arms, she wished their perfect Labor Day weekend could last forever.

Without saying a word, Rick bent down and kissed her on the back of the neck. The kiss left her giggling, but she knew what it meant—their afternoon break was about to be over. Happy, in love, wanting to touch, Amy reached out and traced the line of Rick's shorts against the stiffish blond hairs on his leg.

"Time's up!" he announced, and gave her a swat on the backside.

Amy let out a moan. "Five more minutes, what can it hurt?"

"No way, Faye, that's all you get."

She rolled over. "Are you going to be this mean after we're married?"

"Worse," Rick said, laughing, "lots worse."

Downstream a dozen feet, Clyde was already on his feet, throwing punches at Amy's little brother Ben and shouting, "Up and at 'em, you slug!"

Amy squinted at the skinny sixteen-year-old whose outline was bouncing around in front of the sun. Who'd have guessed, leaving Salt Lake City at six A.M., that they'd end up hiking with a total stranger? A hyperactive teenager, no less, who said he was from Santa Monica, California. All angles and freckles, with hair red as the Navajo sandstone, Clyde looked to Amy like someone who hadn't quite grown into himself.

Behind his back, Rick called him "a one-man band." His sound effects were classic—a metal canteen banging on his pack frame, a permit flapping in the breeze, one knee popping in syncopation.

"Me and Clyde are gonna lead this time," Ben piped up as he brushed the red dust off his backpack.

"Sounds cool," Clyde agreed. "The dynamic duo, huh? Us little fellers."

2

Amy had to laugh. Clyde was taller than any of them.

Finally on her feet, she worked her arms through the straps of her pack, tightened everything, then cinched up the webbing on the hip belt. She was glad she didn't have to carry Rick's pack. They'd allowed half a day to get to their camping site in the Narrows, a second day to continue on down to the mouth. Meals for three had turned out to be bulkier than she'd expected.

It took another minute to get Ben organized, then they all took off again, Amy smiling happily as she fell in alongside Rick.

So far the approach had been dry and hot and sagebrushy, a bit of a letdown, but they'd soon be dropping into the twisty, snakelike passages of the Narrows proper. That was another world. It was hard to believe the storybook stream they were following was the North Fork of the Virgin River, muscled agent of the amazing erosion that lay ahead. Patiently, persistently, over millions of years, the river had carved a deep, paper-thin canyon through the layers of red sandstone. In the literature they'd picked up at the Visitor's Center, the Zion Narrows was called one of nature's most dramatic pieces of sculpture.

"Are you okay?" Rick asked her now as he stopped to shift his pack.

She nodded. "Ben's the one who'll wear himself out."

Rick hrrumphed. "He's almost twelve, isn't he? The kid's in his prime."

Amy glanced ahead at her brother in his moldering sneakers and top-heavy backpack, taking big steps to keep up with Clyde. Their mother had had fits about her bringing him. "Twelve miles from one end to the other? He'll never make it," she'd predicted. So far he was doing great.

"You tired today or what?" Rick asked, giving Amy a friendly bump with his elbow. "What time'd you get to bed?"

"Past midnight. I didn't leave the zoo until eleven, then I had to pack, so four hours of sleep was *it*."

"No wonder you're dragging."

"Look, R. C., you're talking to a woman who's in shape."

His eyebrows jumped.

She grinned, shoving him away. "Stop leering at me! I know I worry too much about Ben, but he always seems so much younger than he is. I don't want to push him too hard."

"Well, you're the one who makes the promises, then has to keep 'em."

They'd been over it once already, why there were four of them tramping across the plateau instead of two. Of course, with Clyde they hadn't had much

4

choice. They'd found him sitting forlornly at the first stream crossing, just beyond the Chamberlain's Ranch gate. Alone.

"Jeez, am I glad to see you guys!" he'd shouted right off.

Amy could see why the backcountry ranger suggested he attach himself to another party. His cargo shorts were straight off the rack. He also wore a pair of expensive new streambed shoes and was toting—of all things—a vintage Boy Scout canteen. Even his eagerness labeled him as a newcomer to wilderness hiking.

"I'm Clyde McKenzie," he'd said, friendly as a pup, explaining how his hiking buddy, Jason, had been flattened by the flu just that morning. Two hours later he and Ben were in the lead.

Amy easily matched her stride to Rick's, filling her lungs with fresh air and loving the workout. The sun and the sky, a rich decorator blue, were enough to inspire poetry.

"Why'd you wait until midnight to do your packing?" asked Rick.

"I couldn't leave the zoo until I finished charting, and I wanted to make sure Rambo was eating. You should have seen his fuzzy little face this week."

Rick grinned. "They give you the title of Relief Zoo Keeper and suddenly you're indispensable, day or night. 'Amy, get over here! The hippo's hyper.' "

5

She clutched her stomach. "The baboon's got a bellyache!"

"I don't know about that vet. I think he takes advantage—"

"Rick!" she cut him off. "I just adore Rambo." What did he think, anyway? She'd raised the kodiak from the incubator when he was a wiry, four-pound cub sucking on her fingers. They'd bonded, for heaven's sake!

"Did that checklist I gave you help any?"

"No. I wasted an extra ten minutes last night looking for it. I never did find the dumb list."

"Amy, you flake! I never knew anyone so disorganized."

"I'm the first to admit it," she said sweetly, batting her eyes.

He blew into his cheeks, making what she called his God-help-us face, but they ended up hugging—no easy maneuver in backpacks.

We *are* different, Amy thought, sidestepping to avoid a clump of sage. Rick was capable, precise, motivated, organized to the max. She was none of those things. He was also the best-looking guy she'd ever met, with sandy coloring to match the desert. She was plain as mustard. When he took her in his arms, however, none of their differences mattered.

Amy looked up to see Clyde waving his map and yelling. "We're dropping down. Outcroppings ahead."

"Outcroppings ahead," echoed Ben an octave higher.

Earlier, Amy had tried seeing the landscape through Clyde's eyes. How would miles of red soil and the semi-arid Markagunt Plateau look to someone raised on the ocean? Scrub junipers weren't palm trees.

Now, looking past Clyde and Ben, her eyes following the course of the river, she spotted hawks soaring and a darker bird, a buzzard maybe, who'd left his perch in a dead cottonwood and was out scavenging lunch.

The country here is so vast, she thought. Vast and exposed, as if the sky in southern Utah slammed directly into the earth without the buffering softness of deciduous trees.

Amy hooked a wisp of hair behind her ear, wishing she knew more about the rivers crossing this plateau. *Deformation* was the word the guidebook used in explaining how the Narrows came to be. It was a nice word, she decided, now that she was about to experience its results firsthand. It had a solid geological sound that suggested eons of time: *form*ation, *de*formation, the wrinkling and tipping that enabled gulleys, finally canyons, to form.

Amy felt prickles on her scalp. The idea of following the river and dropping into a canyon some 2,000 feet below the surface was suddenly terribly exciting. The knifelike Narrows, still being cut through the rock after thirteen million years, was about to swallow them up!

Amy smiled, realizing she couldn't imagine that many years without doing damage to her brain. It was relativity again, wasn't it? Time was always perceived in relation to what you were doing, or in relation to what was going on. In early June, the summer had stretched ahead like an eternity. Now it was over and people were already sending wedding gifts.

How will it be? she wondered, her mind leaping back across geologic ages, to really belong to another person? To be married, of all things!

"Mrs. Rick Chidester," she'd written on the phone pad at the zoo hospital (a hundred times), varying it only with "Amy Diane Chidester, DVM," the degree in veterinarian medicine to be added at some future date. She hoped.

Amy hoisted her pack from underneath, held it a minute, then let the weight settle onto her hips and shoulders again. She shivered in the full sun, remembering the night two months ago when she'd made up her mind to say yes, when she'd stayed awake until dawn weighing every little flaw in Rick's character. As if she were perfect herself.

"Amy, are you there?"

She jumped to find Rick peering in her face.

"What were you thinking about so hard?"

Her cheeks grew warm. If Rick had doubts, he never admitted them.

"I was thinking about marrying you," she said, feeling only slightly dishonest.

He gave her a pleased look before admitting, "Yeah, me, too. You think you'll like being married to an investment counselor, even if he's still a graduate student?"

Amy blew a strand of hair out of her eyes. She knew almost nothing about the work Rick did in his father's firm, but she was learning. Stocks had always dipped or soared by magic as far as she was concerned.

"So long as I can help support us," she told him after a minute. "You know how much I love my job with the baby animals."

"Your dad says he won't give you away unless you promise to get your degree. Sounds like he means it."

"Oh, he does! Not to worry"—Amy's chin came up—"I can do both."

She fell in behind Rick at a place where the riverbank narrowed. She listened as he went on talking about graduate school, but the heat was starting to get to her and she found herself wishing for some cloud cover. Without breaking stride she lifted the heavy French braid off her neck and deftly clipped

9

it on top of her head. The breeze reaching her neck and underarms felt good. Next time they stopped, she'd change into her pink tank top.

Ahead and across the river on a sandy terrace, Ben and Clyde were hunched over looking at something. Clyde was throwing his arms around and swinging his rear end, and Ben was shrieking with laughter.

Rick shielded his eyes. "What are they up to now?"

"Who knows? Old Ben adores strangers."

"Amy!" hollered Ben. "Guess what? We chased a lizard over here. He's puttin' on a show."

"The lizard's doing push-ups!" Clyde yelled. "Never saw anything so interesting in my life."

Amy glanced sideways at Rick and they broke out laughing. Clyde was only a few years younger than she was, but he was crazier than Crackerjacks.

"Maybe they'll regress completely out of sight," Rick said.

"Hey, Bud, that's my baby brother you're talking about."

Abruptly, he reached out and pulled Amy in for a kiss. She held him there, tasting the strawberry Chapstick he'd borrowed from her earlier.

"I think we lucked out with Clyde, don't you?" she whispered as they drew apart. "Once we catch up with the Dwyers, there'll be six of us—seven, if he hangs around—and zero chance to be alone."

10

Clyde and Ben came splashing back across the stream, then hurried ahead to keep their lead.

"He's actually kind of cute," Amy said in a teasing voice.

"Clyde? Kind of dorky, you mean."

"No, he's so dorky he's cute." She hoisted her pack back in place. "He reminds me of that hyrax we had at the zoo. Remember Coney . . . with the big teeth?"

Rick didn't have a chance to reply. A terrifying yelp from Ben jerked them to a stop.

"Rattler!" screamed Clyde.

Rick's arm flew out across Amy. At the same time Clyde grabbed Ben and whirled him around the way you'd play "statues" on a summer night.

Rick was out of his pack before Amy could think what to do.

"Ben!" she cried, running toward him. He rammed into her stomach almost hard enough to knock her down. "Are you okay?" She pulled him back by the hair. *"Are you?"*

He nodded against her.

"Hold it"—Clyde shouted—"he's taking off. Oh my hell, look! He's a monster! Six feet, big as my arm."

The snake pulled itself into a clump of brush. Thrusting its head straight up, it watched them, its tongue forking in and out, in and out.

Amy's whole body had gone clammy, but her

training surfaced quickly once they were safe. "Is it a rattler? Are you sure?"

Clyde gave a shrill laugh. "I heard it! It was right there in front of us, a pile of snake flesh. Man, that gives you the creeps!"

Rick's face had gone a bright red, but now he edged closer, a rock in each hand. "Keep back, you guys, I'm gonna kill that sucker!"

"Wait—" Amy cried.

"Get outa the way!"

Ben danced forward, his eyes wide, eager.

Then the whirring and rattling began and the hair stood on Amy's arms.

"You don't have to kill it now!" she begged. "Let it go!"

But Rick was already heaving a rock at the rattle-snake.

"Missed!" shouted Ben.

The head disappeared from sight, but the rattling grew furious.

Swearing, Rick pounded another rock into the brush. The snake struck, its length a flash of anger that threw them into each other trying to get away.

"Leave it *alone*!" Amy screamed. Why wouldn't he stop? He was running around like a madman. The rattler, making *S*'s in the dirt with frantic speed, was pulsing with more fear than venom.

A second later, Rick pushed past Amy with a

head-sized slab of sandstone that took both hands to lift.

"It's against the law killing rattlesnakes!" she yelled at his back, her heart pounding. She whirled to face Clyde. "Can't you stop him?"

But Rick had already lobbed the big rock at the rattler. She heard the thud, heard her fiancé's exultant yell.

"You got him that time!" whooped Ben.

Amy covered her face and turned away. She was nineteen years old, a grown woman about to be married, but there was no way she could keep from bursting into tears.

2

Hiking the Zion Narrows, Clyde quickly discovered, meant getting and staying wet. If you're not walking right in the river, he'd tell Jason, you're crossing it every few minutes. In and out, in and out. You wade awhile, then step up on a gravel bar. In again, then out on a rocky slope.

Hiking the Zion Narrows, Clyde quickly discovered, meant getting and staying wet. If you're not walking right in the river, he'd tell Jason, you're crossing it every few minutes. In and out, in and out. You wade awhile, then step up on a gravel bar. In again, then out on a rocky slope.

Crazy!

"I can feel my feet aging," Clyde muttered as another bank disappeared and they were forced into the water. "What a pity! Ninety-year-old toes on this devilishly handsome body—"

Amy laughed outright, a great sound after her bad mood over the rattler.

Clyde carefully made his way across the algae-slick rocks, planting his wading stick before each step. Naturally he was tempted to detail the full range of his aches and pains—if that's what it took

14

to make Amy feel better—but he didn't want to sound like a wimp. Besides, he was busy trying to avoid Ben, who was weaving around and grabbing onto whoever was near. It took real concentration to keep from sliding into the drink.

Checking his watch, Clyde was surprised to find it was after four. Rick had said they'd catch up with the Dwyers before they got to The Forks, their campsite, but they hadn't seen a soul. Actually, Clyde didn't care if they never joined up with Rick's neighbors. He was having the hike of a lifetime. Sinking deeper and deeper into the dark passages of the Narrows was exciting beyond all his expectations.

"Utah's Supreme Wilderness Experience," claimed the brochure. What an understatement! Words didn't even come close. Everywhere he looked there were sights that took his breath away: chunky, kitchen-size boulders strewn about like dice; glistening wall gardens of moss and trailing fern; blazing red sandstone, looking warm and smooth, but cold and grainy when you touched it. And hemming them in from either side, cliffs that rose from the riverbed like skyscrapers. *Claustrophobia City!* There were places, Amy had told him, that Paul Bunyan could touch both sides of the canyon at once.

Clyde kept glancing up to make sure there was still a sky overhead, the thin blue ribbon that snaked along between canyon rims.

Jason, old buddy, you're not going to believe any of this! A person would have to *be* here, would have to look up at the towering red walls and scream, "They're coming down on me!"—the way Ben did—to know what it was like.

The canyon had deepened fast once they dropped into the actual Narrows. In fact, the whole atmosphere grew shivery as sunlight crept higher up the cliffs and shade took over the bottoms. In places where water seeped from the rocks and moss carpeted the walls, the air was downright chilly.

"Yeeech, it smells funny in here," Ben said, wrinkling his nose as they came out of the water again. He was starting to sound tired.

"It's supposed to," Amy snapped impatiently. "The terrain's different. It's supposed to smell wet and dank on a river bottom."

"Sounds are different, too, have you noticed?" asked Rick. "Canyon acoustics. They magnify some sounds, muffle others. Weird, huh?"

Clyde had noticed. Their voices, water splashing as they walked, loose rock tink-tink-tinking down, from a thousand, two thousand feet . . .

When they'd stop hiking to take pictures of the desert varnish or a shaft of sunlight, the quiet was just plain spooky.

As the gravel bank petered out, Rick went splashing back into the water at full speed. Ben and Amy followed, but gingerly, and Clyde brought up the rear.

"Are you still worrying about your friend?" Amy asked as she searched for a footing with her pole.

"Yeah," Clyde said, "poor old Jason. What if he needs a doctor and can't find one in that dumb little town?" Suddenly he slipped and had to grab on to Amy. "Oops, sorry! Clumsy Clyde here."

"It's okay, we're all gonna get soaked."

"Anyway," he rattled on, "if one of us had to get sick, it should have been me."

"Oh come on. Why you?"

"You'd have to know Jason. He's the big jock—champion surfer and all that. I can't ride a skateboard, let alone a surfboard. My old man always said if there was a hole, I'd be the one to fall in it."

Amy giggled. Clyde wished he could tell her what else was bothering him. He wasn't sure his best friend would have gone off and left *him*. They'd had a fight about it, with Jason shouting through bleached lips that they'd planned this trip too long, that he'd kill Clyde if he didn't go ahead.

"Yeah . . . I'm here and my best friend's back there in that crummy motel throwing up his toenails."

Rick spoke up. "He'd never make it with the flu. You wouldn't want him along."

"I guess. But he felt terrific yesterday, you know?

17

This morning? Bam! When he dropped me off all he wanted was a bed."

"Glad I didn't get the flu!" cried Ben.

Amy swung around and tickled him. "Me, too."

Their shoes made squeaky sounds coming up out of the cold water and onto another bank. When Amy waited and made room for Clyde to walk beside her, he decided she still wasn't speaking to Rick. He hated being with people when they were fighting.

There was no conversation at all as they made their way across the next difficult ledges. A little farther on, they were confronted with huge, room-size blocks that had been torn from the wall by gravity—an act of erosion that left a perfect arch halfway up the cliff. A pea-green pool had formed in front of the boulders and blocked their way.

Rick probed the pool as far as his stick would reach. "It's deep. Either we rock climb or we swim."

Ben stuck out his tongue. "Grrrross! I wouldn't swim in that stuff."

In the end they had to boost Ben and each other to climb over the barricade. Their hands got sandpapered pink, but with laughing references to climbing Annapurna and K-2, and with a little coaxing, they got across.

Straight, easy trail stuff next. Clyde fell back with Ben, where he could take his time gazing up at the cliffs. In places the walls overhead seemed almost to converge. It was dizzying having an ant's perspective and he couldn't get enough of it.

They hadn't gone a dozen more yards, Amy leading, when Rick grabbed her by the shoulders and yelled, "Snake!" at the top of his lungs.

Amy let out a scream and left the ground.

Clyde plowed backward into Ben—knocked him down, then pulled him up again—all before he heard Rick laughing his head off and knew there hadn't been any snake.

"Richard Chidester!" Amy shrieked. "Are you out of your mind?"

Rick was still howling, collapsed against the cliff. "Your face," he choked, "it was worth the whole trip!"

"You—you stupid jerk! Why'd you do that?"

"Jerk! Hey, come on! Where's your sense of humor?"

"Where's your sense?" she shot back.

His face sobered fast when she pushed past him and took off down the canyon doing the four-minute mile.

Clyde brushed the sand off Ben, handed him the walking stick he'd dropped, then unclipped his own pack and eased it back a bit—something to do. For sure he didn't know what to say.

"Can you believe her going into orbit like that?" Rick asked like some kind of innocent. "What's wrong with her today?"

Clyde could have given him a clue.

Behind him, Ben was tugging on the pocket of his shorts. "People aren't supposed to hike alone," he said when Clyde turned around. "Something could happen."

Clyde rubbed Ben's head. "She'll be okay," he said.

Rick had already dropped his pack and was rotating his shoulders, his arms. "Okay—so, Clyde! Why don't you go ahead and catch up with her? I'll buddy up with Ben awhile, give her a chance to cool off. I sure don't need her on my case about another rattlesnake."

Ben opened his mouth to object, but Rick was right there with good news. "Come on, we'll split a candy bar, take a rest." The look Ben gave Clyde was pure resignation and he left feeling sorry for the kid.

"Maybe I'd rather be alone," he crabbed under his breath. "Maybe I don't want to catch up with her. Does anyone bother to ask? No!"

Ten minutes later he found Amy sitting on a rock, murder in her eyes.

"He makes me so mad sometimes!"

Clyde grinned. "I nearly punched him out myself."

She shot him a grateful look. "Could we please talk about something else besides Rick?"

"Sure."

"Okay."

Amy stood and they started walking again. What did she have in mind? he wondered. Panic wrapped itself around his tongue when he realized he'd have to provide half the conversation now.

"Uh—" he began, remembering dumb things people asked him, "well—uh—what do you want to be when you grow up?"

She burst out laughing. "As if you give a fig! Okay, but you tell me first. Go ahead, you first."

"What do I want to be?" he repeated slowly, squinting up at the short section of jet trail he could see between the cliffs. "I'll say . . . a pilot."

"Really?"

"No, not really, though I like the idea of all that freedom up there."

"Me, too."

"I've thought of about a hundred things I could do, you know? Here in Utah with all these rocks I think I'll be a geologist. I change my mind every day. Mostly"—he hesitated—"mostly, I want to be a storyteller."

He waited for a reaction, then said, "Well, you asked me."

"No, I love it, honest! I'm just wondering how you get to . . . you know, *be* one."

"You tell a bunch of stories."

She smiled again, reminding him of those sports catalog girls who grin all the way through their hairy wilderness treks. Someone ought to tell girls about smiling, he thought, how it's such an improvement.

"Actually," he went on, "a lot of storytellers are librarians. My mom's a librarian, so I come by it naturally. She says I was born in the stacks."

They were back in calf-deep water for a stretch, then onto a gravel bar that humped up in the middle of the stream.

"How about you?" he asked after they'd quit squealing. The water was getting colder all the time. "You gonna be something when you grow up?"

"First, I get married. In five weeks. Oh my gosh, I guess I'll have to make up with Rick if I'm gonna marry him."

"Good idea. Then what?"

"Work and school both. I work at the zoo hospital now. I help the vet take care of newborns, assist giving shots, stuff like that. I end up doing everything, actually. I even get stuck hosing out cages sometimes."

"No wonder. I mean, no wonder you got ticked off back there."

Amy glared at him as if *he*'d killed the snake. "People don't respect the ecological balance. I get so mad! It's not our job to wipe out the other species, and I thought Rick knew better."

"Most guys I know would kill a rattler if they had the chance," Clyde said. "Don't you think?"

"That's the trouble."

End of conversation on that subject. End of conversation, *period*, Clyde thought a minute later. He sneaked a sideways look trying to read her face, but couldn't.

"I guess I should wait and not make Rick walk with Ben," she said finally, turning around to see if they were coming. "I'm being kind of nasty."

"Aw, they'll be all right. He said they'd take a break. Ben looked like he needed one." He wasn't eager to swap her for Ben now that they were talking.

As the canyon switched directions, the shadows on one side deepened. High on the opposite cliff, tans and oranges were ablaze in the sun, overlaid with dark stains that spilled down from the rim like blood. There were black splotches and streaks everywhere: Mother Nature cleaning out her paintbrush, it seemed to Clyde.

"I wish we had time just to look," Amy said. "We'll never make it to The Forks at this rate."

"Who cares? If we take our time, they'll have dinner ready."

"The Dwyers? Dreamer! They're not the type. I mean, they're nice and all that, but they're not the type who'd have a big, blazing campfire made up with coffee on the coals."

"Shucks."

"They weren't exactly wild about doing this hike," Amy said, looking up at him. "It was Neale's therapist who said she had to choose the next family vacation, and this is what she picked. Can you believe it?"

"Who's Neale?"

"Their daughter. She's fourteen. And a little bit"— Amy wrinkled her nose—"strange. And even less outdoorsy than her parents."

"Hold it a minute," Clyde handed her his walking stick. "I want a picture of those spires while they're still in the sun."

Clyde held his camera vertically, then horizontally, then vertically again. "This place really blows me away," he said, peering into the viewfinder.

"Oh, me too. Sometimes I feel like crying, it's so beautiful in here. You know what I mean?" She sounded embarrassed to be saying it. "It's just so . . . so beautiful!"

"You need to work on your vocabulary."

She laughed.

"Do you see a funny old geezer up there in the rock?" Clyde asked as he advanced his film. "Farther over." He pointed. "He's hunched up laughing about something. Straight out of Charles Dickens—see him?"

He put his camera back in the pocket of his shorts, but Amy continued staring. "Yeah, there's one next

24

to him. Hey, there are *two* geezers up there!"

"No no no! The one on the right's a woman."

Amy drew back. "How can you tell?"

"Look at her mouth. She's talking up a storm."

He didn't get the rise out of Amy he expected, just a squinty-eyed look, but a minute later she swung out her arms and smacked him square across the stomach with her walking stick. Her "excuuuuuse me" didn't sound a bit sincere.

Naturally he parried, after which they smacked sticks like fencers. They ended up getting wet when Amy ran splashing and screaming back into the water.

They tried to get serious about hiking again, but with all the slipping and sliding and laughing it was hard. The stream bottom had turned to pure slime. Constantly they had to grab hands.

Suddenly Clyde realized how much fun he was having with Amy. He hoped he wouldn't fall in love with her. He was always falling in love. By the time they came out of the Narrows Sunday afternoon, they'd say good-bye and never see each other again.

"Want to try for another adjective?" Amy asked a little later.

"Has anyone said *beautiful*?"

"Okay, smart ass, how about *whimsical*?"

"Good word," Clyde agreed. It was a word his mother would have chosen. Suddenly he wished she were here to see all this whimsy—the hobgoblins of erosion, ripples and swirls that turned sandstone into hot caramel topping, real enough to make his mouth water. His mother's life was so boring. All she ever did was work.

Clyde was about to say "pockmarked," having identified a real bad case of acne high up on the cliff, when they came to a cave at water level that was so perfect it might have been hollowed out with an ice cream scoop.

It was dark and cold inside, the size of a double garage with a leaky roof. Drops from the overhang fell on their heads and went sliding down their arms.

"I wonder where the springs are," Amy said in a whisper. "There must be springs for the rocks to ooze like this." She hugged her bare arms.

"This place would make a great horror movie. Can't you just see some guy tied to his walking stick in here? It gets to be night and all these bats come out—" Clyde made a high-pitched whine and flapped his wings over Amy.

She shrank away crying, "Spare me, Vincent Price!"

They got even sillier yelling and making echoes. When Amy finally got Clyde to shut up, they stood and listened to their noises bounce off the overhang and spiral away—echoes on top of echoes.

"Medieval!" Clyde was glad to get back to the stream and the vertical walls that looked as if they might come down on him any minute.

He was also glad now that he'd taken the ranger's advice. A person could really get the creeps in here alone. He hadn't mentioned it to Amy, but he suspected a trip through the Narrows came with something like built-in terror for first-timers. It was all so alien, so still. Even the canyon wrens had quit singing as the afternoon faded.

They looked back to see if Rick and Ben were in sight. Not yet. Clyde unfolded his map and with a finger traced the river as it gradually curved south, past the falls, to a place people called The Forks. There the Deep Creek joined the North Fork of the Virgin; on the little peninsula of land between the rivers they planned to spend the night.

"So"—Clyde tapped the map—"we camp here, then we continue on down to the mouth tomorrow."

"Right. Unless Ben holds us up, we should be out by late afternoon."

They decided the falls, a short distance ahead, would be a good place to stop and wait.

Putting away the map, Clyde checked the sliver of sky overhead. Still clear. Only a few fluffy clouds since morning—a good sign. And so far the river itself was a pussycat, hardly more impressive than the "crick" that crossed his grandma's pasture in Nebraska.

"Just for the record," he asked Amy, "where's the point of no return on this trip?"

"We already passed it. You're committed."

27

"Oh great!" he answered. "Good thing I didn't want to go back."

A minute later they were forced into the first really deep spot in the river. The water was up to Amy's shorts and the loaf-shaped rocks were slippery as sea jelly. Clyde's ankles were turning every which way. Somehow, by hanging on and bending each other's fingers, they made progress toward a skinny little bank developing on the other side. That time it wasn't the cold so much as the current that took Clyde's breath away. He was glad to get out of the water again, glad also when Amy took the lead so she couldn't see how hard he was shaking.

Clyde studied Amy's body as she walked ahead of him—the tan legs, the good shoulders, mostly bare in the pink tank top, the wispy hairs at her neck.

Even doing a splendid wilderness trek, you've got to have sex on the mind, he reprimanded himself. She's engaged, you pervert! She wouldn't look at you if she wasn't.

Well, he could dream. That's how he spent most of his time, anyway. Someday, if he was lucky, he might have a girl worrying about him the way Amy did Rick, sneaking kisses and soft looks. What would it be like?

Amy fell silent, too, walking along, and the worried look returned to her face. Each time she swung around, he knew she was hoping to see Rick. They needed to be alone together, then maybe they could kiss and make up. Why did people have to let things get so complicated, anyway?

Before long, Clyde heard the sound of the falls and knew his time with Amy was nearly up. He wondered, fool that he was, what Rick would do if he decided not to give her back.

There was no more picture taking beyond the falls as evening took over the Narrows and a breeze set Clyde's permit tag twirling. All traces of the sunny afternoon were gone.

If Rick hadn't insisted they were close to the junction where the Deep Creek and the North Fork joined, Clyde would have voted to make camp on a rock. He hurt all over. They were hiking at about half the speed and with about a tenth of the vigor as earlier, and it wasn't nearly as easy negotiating the stream with Ben hanging on to his rear pocket.

Finally, abruptly, the North Fork Canyon—no wider at that point than fifteen feet—opened out into a broader, lighter area. They could see trees and grass again. It was the confluence, all right.

"Green stuff!" Clyde yelled happily. "I'm gonna be homesick."

He could see now why everyone called this place The Forks. Seen from the air, the deep canyon cuts would form the letter Y. They'd be making camp on the triangle of land between the arms of the letter.

Wading across the North Fork, Clyde could see the Deep Creek coming in at an angle, could see how the river swelled where the two became one down-canyon. The triangular peninsula of land had apparently built up over the years, with sandy terraces stepping up to a high place, a grassy mound that butted against the cliff ten feet or so above stream level.

Suddenly the four of them were shouting and grabbing each other. All was forgiven as Rick kissed Amy on top of the head. She nearly fell in trying to kiss him back.

"About time we got here!" grumbled Ben, his tongue hanging out like some dead critter's. He could hardly drag his feet through the water.

The point of land offered beaches first, then brush, saplings, and slightly larger trees. What a great spot! Clyde wished Jason could see it—the sun-tipped trees shivering against the backdrop of towering cliffs. He'd have to take pictures in the morning.

Suddenly Clyde found himself sniffing the air.

Sweet shades of Saturday night! It was like strolling past the hamburger stand at the pier.

"Civilization!" he shouted. "I can smell onions!"

"It's the Dwyers!" Amy whooped. "You guys, we made it."

3

Neale was stretched out on a sleeping bag on the sand—eyes closed, headset in place over her curly hair. Even with all the noise they were making coming out of the water, she didn't look up. She just lay there in her big shirt and flowered shorts, swinging one pale leg to the beat.

"That girl's jivin'," Clyde said to no one in particular.

Typical! thought Amy, stepping up to the next sandy terrace, loosening her straps as she went.

Expecting to see Neale's parents, she was surprised when the person chopping wood near the cliff straightened and turned out to be a slender man with a mustache. When she saw the old-style backpacking stove, she realized it was someone else's dinner they'd been smelling. She felt cheated.

She dropped her pack, pulled her tank top away

from her sweaty skin. The cool air felt like a dusting of talcum on her back. Looking around for the Dwyers, she rubbed the back of her neck. It irritated the heck out of her that Neale would just lie there and ignore them.

Amy turned around in time to see Rick take off a shoe and dribble dirty water over Neale's legs.

That got Neale up and swatting with both hands. "I *know* you're here," she screeched.

"So where's your dad, Pruneface?"

"In a minute. I wanta finish this song."

"Now!" Rick insisted as he planted a wet sock on her legs. Having been Neale's babysitter in the days when she was manageable, he still teased her every chance he got.

Amy dug in her pack for a water bottle. Tipping it up for a drink, she saw a woman coming toward her, pushing aside branches and smiling. She was tanned, dark-haired, fortyish maybe, someone who looked okay in a sweatshirt and jeans.

"Are you the people Neale's been expecting?" she called to Amy.

"We thought so. Are the Dwyers here somewhere?"

"Didn't she tell you? They decided to go on to the Grotto."

Amy moaned. "Where's that?"

"It's a popular spot for overnights, about an hour down-canyon." The woman bent over the fry pan, gave the potatoes and onions a quick stir, then came on to where Rick had joined Amy and was stripping off his pack.

"I'm Audrey," she said as she put out her hand. "He's Steve."

Rick followed suit, introducing Amy and the others by first names.

"We had already set up when they got here," Audrey went on. "We came in down Deep Creek from Navajo Lake. Neale's parents said they didn't want to crowd us, but honestly"—she shrugged good-naturedly—"it would have been fine."

The man named Steve came over next, swinging his hatchet and carrying a plastic bag full of wood. He dropped both, wiped his hands on his chino pants. "They took off about four, didn't they?" he asked Audrey, who nodded.

Rick exhaled noisily, swore under his breath. "Wish they hadn't done that."

"The girl was worn out by the time they got this far," Steve said, "close to tears, I think. She pretty much refused to go on."

Amy pushed her bangs off her forehead and held them there a minute. "So they want us to meet them at the Grotto?" She swung around to face Rick. "You think we can make it?"

"I can't go another inch!" Ben was listening, even though he'd collapsed on the ground.

"Well, you may have to," snapped Rick.

"I got too many blisters." Ben sat up and looked to Clyde for support, but Clyde was into his pack, pointedly minding his own business.

"I can't believe this," Rick said. "Why would the Dwyers make plans with us if they weren't going to—"

"Why'd they leave you here?" Amy asked Neale, who came up carrying her sleeping bag and headset.

"Because!" Neale's lip shot out.

"Because why?"

"They thought you'd be here lots earlier, then I'd go on down with you. Mostly they were tired of hearing me bitch."

"So *we* get to hear you bitch," Rick muttered. "Great!"

Neale, her back to Clyde, started making motions, mouthing "Who's he?"

Amy ignored her and looked over Rick's shoulder at the map he was studying.

"It would take us an hour"—he said—"at least that, maybe more. It's after six now—"

"Oh, let's stay here," Amy said. "We'd end up making dinner in the dark, and we're already crabby. . . ."

"Look, Amy, you don't know Hal Dwyer like I do. They're expecting us. He wanted to talk about a bond portfolio Dad worked up for him, and I said we'd do it tonight."

34

"You did? You were going to talk business . . . in the Narrows?"

"Sure, why not?"

Amy threw up her hands. "Don't you ever let down?"

"Isn't anybody interested in what *I* think?" Neale asked.

"No!" from Rick.

Glaring at both of them, Neale slung her nylon sleeping bag around her neck like a fur piece and stalked off, sandals and shirttail flapping.

Amy had to laugh. They weren't being fair to Neale, but right now being fair was the least of her worries.

Audrey took her big spoon and went back to stirring potatoes, but Steve just stood there studying the ground, hands in his pockets. He was an interesting-looking man with a mustache that was grayer than his hair. He had a generous smile and bright, intelligent eyes. Amy could picture him in front of a class of graduate students answering questions about dolomites.

When he looked up at Rick, he said, "I think I'd stay if I were you."

Amy sensed that he wasn't comfortable telling Rick what to do, but felt he should anyway.

"Early morning might be safer," he went on. "Hiking another hour this time of day, especially

35

without eating"—he hooked a thumb toward Ben—"you might end up carrying him. I've been through here once or twice, and it gets dark fast this time of year. The volume of water's also two thirds greater from here on—"

Rick bent over and took his time retying his shoe. Amy noticed how the pink had crept up his neck and into his cheeks. He didn't know what to do any more than she did.

Suddenly she wanted to put her arms around him and tell him she loved him. Things weren't turning out right, but it wasn't his fault.

"Does it matter if we all camp in one spot?" she said. "We have enough food for Neale. You know we always bring too much."

Rick didn't answer. Instead he got up and headed across to the Deep Creek side, where he stood—legs apart, hands on hips—looking down at the darkening Virgin River. She saw his shoulders sag. He was mad and he was disappointed. The Dwyers had been family friends forever, and Rick had promised to show them a great time in the Narrows when he learned they were all going the same weekend. She knew how he felt.

"We drove three hundred miles today to get here from Salt Lake"—Amy told Steve as they stood there—"then the hike on top of it. Rick's exhausted."

36

"I'm sure he'll decide to stay," Steve told her, the unspoken part being "Let him think it over."

His mild manner reminded her of her father and the subtle ways he had of encouraging without telling. Her mother once said he was "passively aggressive." She still wasn't sure what that meant, but advice given with a hug—her dad's way—was always easier to take.

Amy's heart sank when she went down to check on Ben. What he showed her was a bumper crop of red, puffy blisters—on all the toes, both heels, even the balls of his feet. "Oh, Ben," she said, "why didn't you tell me?"

"I did, but you said we had to keep going."

Her eyes stung. "With school starting Tuesday, Mom's gonna kill me!"

"I've got Nupercainal if you want some," Clyde offered. He had the tube in his hands and was doctoring himself. "Feels good, feels numby. Get it, Ben? N-u-m-b, numby?"

"Thanks," Amy said, "we may need it. So where are your Band-Aids, Ben? You'll want some clean socks, dry shoes—" She sat cross-legged on the sand and opened his pack. "Don't worry, I'll get you all fixed up. By morning you'll be rarin' to go again."

His brown eyes were big with doubts, but he nodded and let her fuss.

When Rick came back and said they were staying,

Amy was so glad she wrapped an arm around his leg and kissed his sweaty kneecap. She was acting a little bit like a slave woman, but she didn't care. If he'd wanted to go on, it would have been without Ben and her and there'd have been another fight. She wasn't good at the passive stuff herself.

Rick dropped down beside Amy and pulled off his shoes and socks. They spent the next few minutes comparing damage, until Ben wiggled his leprous toes in Amy's face and got her laughing.

Soon they were howling over everything and nothing. When Clyde pulled up his nose like an English butler's and called them "riff-raff," Rick laughed so hard he fell over. Amy wondered what Audrey and Steve must think of them, but she couldn't stop.

Neale, during all this, sat apart on her sleeping bag, her expression a little like the English butler's. Clyde waved at her once. Playfully. E. T. making contact. Although her mouth twitched slightly, she didn't wave back.

Finally, with things under control and their dinner started, Amy remembered her manners and called out, "Neale, this is Clyde McKenzie from Santa Monica. You're going to like him. Clyde"—looking around until she spotted him opening a can—"this is Neale Dwyer, who took first place in her school's vocal competition. We'll have her sing for us tonight. She's awesomely talented."

Amy then went back to cutting cheese into her spaghetti sauce, humming "My Favorite Things" from *The Sound of Music*.

"Glad to meet you, miss," Clyde said to Neale, bowing low in the continental manner. "The pleasure is indubitably mine."

Amy laughed seeing what agony it was for him to straighten up, but his antics got a smile out of Neale.

4

After dinner Clyde got busy organizing his pack, laying out what he'd need. Before long he was having another imaginary conversation with Jason.

You won't believe how friendly it is sharing a latrine at The Forks. Picture this: one bathroom wall is a cliff. The other is a clear piece of plastic draped over a hiking stick. I mean, you could be mooning and not even know it.

Clyde chuckled. Jason would understand why he was opting for a private place to sleep. This three-sided piece of property suddenly felt more crowded than the Santa Monica beach in July. Besides, hiking the Narrows, according to what he'd read, was supposed to foster a sense of independence. So far he felt like a camp follower.

Clyde looked up to see Ben hobbling toward him, sucking on the remains of a plum. He stopped, heaved the pit across the Deep Creek, waited for it to hit the cliff. Grinning with satisfaction, he wiped his hands on his jeans and came on.

Everyone was wearing long pants now except Neale, who'd complained that her warm-ups were in her dad's pack. She was marching around in Rick's Patagonia jacket, her spindly legs covered with goosebumps.

"Can I go see your cave?" Ben asked. "It's gonna be dark."

"Tell Amy. I'm taking off in one minute."

"What's that you got?" Ben asked.

"A headlamp."

"Oh yeah. Like in the coal mines?"

"Sort of, only this is a sports model. I'll let you wear it up there if you hustle your butt."

"Hey, you got a rope, too—"

Clyde tossed it to Ben. "Seven millimeter rescue rope. Catalog #146B. My friend and I figured we'd take turns carrying it, but you can see who got stuck."

"Heck, we didn't bring any of this stuff."

"Be prepared, that's my motto. You a Scout, Ben?"

"Nope. Hey, Amy—" He limped off on the outsides of his feet to where she and Rick sat on what they were all calling "the beach." The lovers were drinking hot chocolate out of a single cup.

Although Clyde had scouted the sandbar along the Deep Creek earlier, Ben's blisters had kept him from tagging along then. The mini-grotto, as he now thought of it, was comfortably above water level and back from the river the distance of several walking sticks. Steve told him he'd slept there once—"when I was your age," he'd said with a sheepish grin.

When Ben came back with Amy's okay, Clyde adjusted the webbing of the headlamp and let him take the lead up the riverbank.

The cave wasn't more than a hundred yards beyond a rockslide at the bend, but they walked at a snail's pace. Clyde figured Ben was as scared as he was incapacitated, so he let him creep along and didn't say anything.

"Glad we don't have to cross the river and get our feet wet again," Ben called back once.

Finally the trail widened into a broad sandy area and they were there.

"Homey, ain't it?" Clyde said, making like a realtor. "Big ol' tree on the patio, great place for drying socks and stuff. I can arrange a thirty-year mortgage if you think you'll live that long."

Ben giggled, looked around.

Clyde lowered his pack and ducked inside. There wasn't much head room, especially at the back where the cave sloped to nothing. It was deep enough for a man-size sleeping bag, broad enough to sleep three or four.

After propping the light on the sand, they got busy smoothing a place for Clyde's mat and bag.

Clyde set the streambed shoes by the head of his bag, alongside the coil of rope. "Smart to have things handy," he told Ben.

He propped the backpack frame on its side at the bottom of everything else: "To keep out bears."

Ben snickered at the idea of bears in the Narrows.

"Want me to hang your rope in the tree?" Ben asked, having never stopped eyeing it. "That's what I'd do if it was mine."

"Sure. Good thinking. You do it."

Clyde stretched out on his sleeping bag and sighed, wishing like anything some magic could turn Ben into Jason. He remembered the day in his mom's library when Jason and he had sneaked Milky Ways into the viewing room after school. The videotape, "Hiking the Zion Narrows," had merely been an excuse for a food break. They'd ended up watching the documentary three times, then checking it out again, vowing they'd hike that canyon together someday.

Sure enough, one year later they were boarding a plane in L.A., looking like a couple of rock jocks. As planned, they'd borrowed an old Land Cruiser from Jason's uncle in Las Vegas, then taken turns driving it across the desert to Zion Canyon. All that trouble and money—and now Jason sick.

43

"Rick said it was dumb to bring a rope," Ben mentioned as he carefully lowered himself from the bottom branch.

"Yeah, well . . . he would."

Then Ben was sitting on the edge of the sleeping bag, scooping up handfuls of the fine sand and letting it sift through his fingers. Clyde reached down and switched off the light. "Don't talk," he said.

"How come? Why'd you do that? It's too dark."

"I want you to listen. Hear the water? . . . Nice, huh?"

They listened awhile.

"That's all there is. 'The Narrows reduces everything to fundamentals.' That's what the ranger lady said on the videotape. She was right."

What he liked, Clyde supposed, was not just the quiet, but the absence of all the normal noises of his life. No car doors slamming . . . no freeway pollution . . . no wheezing brakes and grinding gears . . . no TV coming from the Alberghetti apartment where the snot-nosed kids had lost the volume knob.

Here, gently flowing water was positively all there was, although the sensations of moving air on the skin came very close to being whispers. His scalp tingled with the thrill of being alone in the Narrows.

"You gonna get scared?" Ben asked.

"Me? Clyde, the brave?" He sat up, swung his

44

feet out onto the sand, "Yeah, I'll probably get scared, but it won't keep me awake."

"Hey, why don't I sleep here with you?" Ben said in a sly voice, as if the idea had just this minute occurred to him. "I'd rather be with you than with *them*." He made a just-kissed-by-a-girl face that left Clyde grinning.

"Grab the lamp, you old tadpole, we better go back for the campfire. They'll be out looking for us."

Amy the conservationist insisted on keeping their campfire small, feeding it with just enough driftwood to keep flames dancing over the coals.

"It's pitch black in this canyon," Audrey kept saying. "Ever see it so dark? There's supposed to be a moon tonight, but it's not shining on us."

The stars were a different story. In what little sky they could see, the stars were brilliant. Ben spent most of his time lying on his back looking straight up at them. "For once," he gloated, "I can count *all* the stars in the sky."

"That's a minimal horizon, all right," Steve said. "*T*-shaped from where I sit."

Rick craned around to study the sky from Steve's angle. "From over here it's a *Y*-shaped sky."

Amy, too, was leaning back on her hands. "I've never gone to sleep under such tiny little strips of sky—ever. Kind of like being at the wrong end of a tunnel, isn't it?"

Rick chuckled. "Yeah. Like, help, somebody! What are we doing down here?"

"Let me out, let me out!" squeaked Ben, clawing the air with both hands.

Audrey called it an "arresting perspective," a phrase Clyde hoped he'd remember for Jason.

"Well, *I*'m not crazy about it," Neale said emphatically. "I mean, you know, I'd feel awful if this was the last sky I ever saw." She looked across the fire at Clyde. "You know what I mean?"

"No," he said, "explain it."

"It's just—well—I used to think about stuff like that all the time." She pulled Rick's jacket over her drawn-up knees. "Like, what if this was my last dinner . . . or my last bubble bath . . . you know? Or the last music I'd hear. I always think of stuff like that." She hugged herself and rocked on the sand. "But then, I'm weird."

Audrey laughed outright. "You're not weird, you're interesting. There's a big difference, you know."

"Oh, yeah, right!" Neale grinned. "I'm interesting, I forgot."

"We'd all feel terrible if this was our last sky," Rick said quietly. "Me especially. I'd never get to marry Amy." He drew her close and she smiled.

Shifting to avoid the smoke, Clyde noticed a sim-

46

ilar look passing between Audrey and Steve just then, a communication so subtle he might have missed it in another time or place. He felt left out. How'd he get in with all these lovers? Such soulful looks belonged on the soaps, didn't they?

Finally, after a little more talk and after failing to get Neale to sing, they all agreed it was bedtime.

The sleeping bags had been laid out earlier—Audrey's and Steve's on the high mound near the cliff, Amy's and Rick's on the beach. Neale was sleeping nearby on an even lower terrace, too close as far as Rick was concerned, too far away in Neale's opinion. Twice Clyde had seen her tug her bag closer to theirs when they weren't looking.

Now, pulling the fire apart with a stick, Steve said, "I think we should talk about what we'll do if it rains during the night."

Rick let out a nervous laugh. "Plans A, B, and C—Get the heck out of here!"

"In the dark?" Ben got up on his knees at such a suggestion. Then his look of alarm turned smug and he said, "We've got the best spot. You guys can all come up to our cave."

Steve reached out and tapped Clyde on the knee. "You'd come back here, of course, with Ben. It wouldn't be safe there."

"Why"—Amy spoke up—"you think it's going to rain?"

"No sign of it," he answered matter-of-factly.

Amy frowned and asked if it was smart for the boys to be sleeping that far away from the rest of them.

"Oh, they'll be fine," Steve said. "That's a nice place and it's up from the water a few feet. But you don't want to fool around down here if it starts raining. The ledge up top where Audrey and I have our bags is safe."

Suddenly everyone grew serious. Although the gentle gurgling of the water was reassuring, Clyde realized they weren't on a plane watching the stewardess pantomime evacuation procedures. They were at the bottom of the Narrows between towering cliffs, practically at stream level. They were vulnerable.

"Look," Steve said "I didn't mean to put a damper on things."

"Have you ever been in a flash flood yourself?" Amy asked.

"No, I haven't . . ."

Ben threw a chip on the fire. It began to smoulder and they all watched in silence to see if it would catch.

". . . but I knew one of the boys who was killed here in 1961," Steve went on. "He was a neighbor, a real nice kid. . . . His death affected me."

Rick whistled. "And you still come in here?"

"This is my sixth trip, but I always think about him. They didn't have a chance, those people, the way it happened."

"How'd it happen?" insisted Ben.

"They were in the narrowest part, a stretch above the Orderville Gulch, when the wall of water hit. No rain, no warning, nothing. It was a cloudburst up on the plateau. You'll know the place when you go through there tomorrow. There's just no high ground anywhere. They were swept away."

"Gosh," Ben said softly. Then, a second later, "What's a wall of water look like?"

Suddenly Audrey's hands went in the air. "Oh Steve, I nearly forgot! How could I forget?" She jumped to her feet, snapped on a light and took off, calling, "Don't anyone go away, I'll be right back."

She returned with a wrapped package, a stack of paper cups, and two cans of Coke. "You have to help us celebrate. It's Steve's birthday." Laughing, she dropped onto the sand and congratulated him with a noisy kiss that started everyone cheering.

"You carried that fancy box all the way in? Two days, and I never saw it?" Steve looked embarrassed and pleased both.

Nodding yes, Audrey popped open a can and poured him a generous serving. She then half filled five more cups and handed them around. "To as many more years," she toasted, "and happier than ever!"

He hooked an arm around her neck and sand-papered her cheek with his stubbly chin.

She made a terrible face, then they all broke into "Happy Birthday to You."

So Neale ended up singing, after all, and there was a lot of whistling and clapping and carrying on.

"Is it a biggie?" Amy asked when she got a chance. "Or a state secret?"

"State secret," Steve said emphatically, giving Audrey a look that meant she shouldn't tell. Behind his head she held up four, and then two, fingers.

They all watched as Steve opened his present and tried on the black-and-white lumberman's shirt. "Soft—" he said. He worked his shoulders "Fits great. Is it wool?"

Then he kissed Audrey, a long sweet one that made everybody look away.

Clyde thought of his dad, who was about Steve's age. It was good to know there were married people in the world who actually *liked* each other.

The celebration was a great way to end the evening. By the time they'd covered the ashes, Amy had finished her hundred or so instructions to Ben— "Sleep in your jeans," and "Don't go wandering around if you wake up early,"and "Don't stay up and talk, you hear?" Already canyon temperatures felt as if they'd dropped to the low fifties.

"Those sleeping bags are gonna feel so good!" Clyde

said as Ben and he started up the Deep Creek, the light bobbing along with their steps. He wore the headlamp this time and carried Ben's pack. The young trees along the bank cast long spooky shadows, as if they'd grown in the dark, and Ben hung on to his rear pocket. For once he didn't mind having Ben hold on to his rear pocket.

5

Amy was wakened by someone stumbling about the latrine. She saw a light through the brush, somewhere close to the cliff, then reached over to see if Rick was still there. Must be Steve, Audrey . . .

She listened for Rick's breathing, but heard only the rustle of fabric as she pulled her arm back into the sleeping bag. The sound of the river covered everything else.

Shifting for the warm spot she'd just left, Amy stared into the dark. No stars now. Just the black night. But Rick was right. From this angle the sky, a shade lighter, resembled a squashed *Y* more than a *T*, as if some giant had stepped on the arms and flattened them out a bit. Was it close to morning? She hoped not—her body didn't feel like morning.

Amy burrowed deeper into the sleeping bag, thinking again how really insignificant the Narrows made her feel. Canyons on such a grand scale had a way of cutting mere humans down to size, of making them feel temporary, as if they were intruders in a sacred place and shouldn't hang around too long. How frightening to be the uninvited guest! In the ecosystem of the Narrows, people counted for less than the rattlesnake Rick had killed.

Amy sighed and let her thoughts go into another fuzzy area.

Sometimes, alone and thinking, she tried seeing her life from the other end, the perspective she'd have at ninety rather than nineteen. By then she'd have some answers. Looking back now, however, she was struck mostly by the dizzying number of years she'd be a married woman—how few she'd been a girl. Nature again, pushing you to get on with it, to get to the next place.

She bunched her jacket into a more comfortable pillow and closed her eyes. Why couldn't a person just stop on a summer like this and graze awhile?

In no time at all Rick was shaking her. "Amy, get up, it's raining!"

She drew up her knees.

"Come on, you can't go back to sleep." He shook her harder. "Neale, roll out!" he yelled over Amy's head. "Storm's movin' in."

Then Amy could hear splats hitting her nylon bag,

but it wasn't raining hard. She squinted against the light Rick shone in her eyes. "Are you getting up? Do we have to?"

"I've *been* up . . . talking to Steve. Yes, you have to."

She felt him scrambling around, stuffing his sleeping bag and zipping his pack. "Shake it, Amy! Steve wants everything up at the top."

Amy sat up, feeling for her jeans. She saw lights moving through the trees, heard shouts, but faintly. A few feet away Neale was dressing in the dark, cussing when she stepped on something.

"Everyone awake?" came Steve's voice through the brush.

"Coming, coming . . ." Amy grumbled.

"This better be a dry run," Rick said as he loaded up his gear.

"What time is it?' Amy asked, but he'd already taken off.

Yanking on her socks, she had an attack of shivers and felt smart to have brought her lined Gortex jacket and not her windbreaker. How could it be raining, anyway? The weather had been perfect, the *forecast* had been perfect.

Ben! Were Ben and Clyde up on that hill with the others? She tried to count the lights—two, plus Rick's bouncing along.

Suddenly she was wide awake, snatching up her

bag, her mat, grabbing the pack with her other hand. Just as suddenly she was aware that a great deal more water was coming down the Deep Creek than when they'd gone to sleep. She couldn't see, but she could hear the difference.

"Neale?" she turned around.

Neale said something, but Amy couldn't catch the words. Now that she was standing, she could hear the North Fork, too—and *it* was louder. With the sky rumbling and rain starting to drive, things were all at once scarier.

"Come on or I'm going without you!"

"Then *go*! I can't find my sandals."

Amy dropped everything and went back, telling herself to stay calm. A little weather wasn't going to spoil their trip. All hikers were warned to take precautions and that's exactly what they were doing— taking precautions.

"But you've got shoes with you, right?" she asked Neale.

"In my pack."

"Forget the sandals, we'll find them later." She loaded Neale's arms with bag and backpack, then pulled her along barefooted to where she'd dropped her own things. Peering through the dark for a glimpse of Ben and Clyde, she saw someone making hurry-up arcs with a light.

"What's the big deal?" Neale grumbled, clinging

to Amy with pinchy fingers. "Cripes, how are we supposed to hurry when we can't even see where we're going?"

"Because it *could* be a big deal if the rain doesn't stop."

Amy ignored the water sliding down her neck as she tried to get up the steep slope to the upper terrace. She was forced to grab onto saplings and brush, finally left her pack below in order to boost Neale, whose bare feet were sliding out from under her. At the top Rick gave them each a hand.

"Not much room," he shouted, "size of a bedroom up here, but Steve says it's safe."

"Where's Ben?" Amy asked first thing. "Haven't they—"

"Not yet," Rick said, pushing air out of Neale's bag.

Audrey stuffed Rick's sleeping bag, then Neale's, into a tan garbage bag along with things of theirs, working fast. "They should be here any minute," she said when she looked up.

"I'd better go up there," Amy said. "Rick, give me the light. Or do you want to go?"

"Hold on." Steve handed Amy's bag over to Audrey, who shoved it in with the rest. "You're right, they ought to be here by now, but I don't want you going anywhere."

"What do you mean? What if they don't show?"

"Just shut up, Amy!" Rick demanded. "Steve knows what he's doing."

"One second," Steve said, a hand on her arm as he ticked off items at Rick. "Is that all the water you've got? So now we'll want food, stove, fuel, anything waterproof—"

Amy stood there, listening but impatient. Who put him in charge, anyway? In his army fatigue jacket—hair plastered flat to his head—he looked exactly like someone in combat.

"No packs," he finished, "there isn't room, we'll hang 'em in the trees down below—"

Then Steve was hooking his light to a side belt loop. "I'm going after the kids myself. Audrey, hand me the rope. I'll get a line across the Deep Creek first. It's not much, but it might save . . . if someone gets swept away by the current . . ."

A line across. What was he talking about?

Rick, shivering there in his sopping wet clothes, didn't look as if he knew what was going on, either.

Amy jumped as thunder crashed overhead. Lightning lit up their point of land and the rocky cliffs like day. She wiped her face on her sleeve and stared off to the right where the Deep Creek came in. *You guys, come on!*

"*You* stay, I'll go," Rick said suddenly. "I don't know what needs doing here, anyway."

Amy's throat tightened as she looked from one to

the other. "Will somebody just go?" she blurted out.

"If the river's broadened out too much in there," Steve said, "it could be a real bitch—"

"Okay, okay," Rick answered, "I can handle it. I'll be up on the bank anyway."

"All right, but take a good stick and keep your ears open. You hear a big roar coming down that canyon, *any* roar, get back here fast. Leave everything. I'll string a rope across to the other side, just above the water line in case you lose footing. Something to grab onto."

Rick nodded impatiently and started off.

"I'll be down there with a light until you get back," Steve shouted after him. "Let the boys know."

"Wait!" Amy said, suddenly scared and grabbing Rick's arm. "No, go—but be careful."

She followed him to the edge and watched him drop down toward the Deep Creek. In the beam of his light, she saw that the gravel bank against the cliff was still half a foot above water.

"And make Ben hurry! He'll fool around if you let him."

Amy squeezed water out of her braid, aware of breathing hard, aware of adrenalin. She stared at the blackness closing in behind Rick and tried in vain to stop shivering.

Another crack of thunder. Then his light disappeared beyond the rockslide and she went back to the others.

Sheet lightning bright as noon showed Audrey making a shelter out of a ground cloth, showed Neale burrowing into the plastic bags, hugging her knees to her chest. Her legs stuck out bare and ghoulish white from Rick's jacket, and the sight of them gave Amy the shakes all over again.

Seconds later, hanging on to each other, Steve and Amy half slid, half stumbled off the mound and down toward the rushing Deep Creek. Once out of the low-growing brush, Steve shone his light up and down the opposite bank. The river looked several times the size it had been when they went to sleep.

"I'll need a good tree over there to tie to," he yelled.

Amy's heart sank seeing their beach in the flashes of lightning. The bottom tier of sand was completely underwater. Neale had been sleeping there just minutes ago.

Amy held the light for Steve as he tied one end of the rope around the base of an ash. Cold rain pelted their heads even as it drilled holes in the sand. Working fast, Steve passed the rope loosely around his waist, then waded in—rope in his left hand, stick in his right.

The Deep Creek was no longer a stream. It was muddy and turbulent—a snarly, angry-looking river. The sight of it sickened Amy.

She watched him struggle out into the current, intent on getting across. Every step was a gamble.

Her own legs grew tense watching him.

That's it, face upstream. . . . Dig in. . . . Come on, Steve!

His rope arm swung wildly as he tried to keep his balance.

"Don't fall!" Amy screamed. She clamped a hand over her mouth as he steadied himself, took another step, another. Suddenly, cartoon fashion, the current spun him completely around. He staggered, grabbed the rope, swung there like a fish on a line.

"You can't make it! Come back!" she shouted, knowing *she* couldn't save him if the rope didn't.

He hauled himself in hand over hand, came out of the river gasping, with water streaming off his legs.

"Need a harness—" His hands shook as he knotted the rope twice, stepped into the loops, tied it at the waist—one swift maneuver. He'd gathered up the slack and was plunging back into the river before Amy could say a word.

She kept the light just ahead of him, swallowing and swallowing. The sound of the river was changing pitch—she could tell. The noise had become a roar.

Oh, Ben, come on, where are you? She craned around trying to see up the Deep Creek. Although sheet lightning danced all around them, the configuration of the canyon made seeing very far impossible.

Steve, when she looked again, was weaving in the

current like a drunk, fighting for every step. Thunder now boomed nonstop. Strobelike lightning made freaky shapes of the cliffs and palsied their hands, turning Steve's movements into an eerie video dance.

He was sliding downcurrent when she saw him let go of the stick and grab the rope with both hands. She lunged forward to pull up the slack and felt the enormous power of the river that was pounding his body, felt the throbbing right through the rope.

Suddenly he had an arm in the air, wildly motioning her back.

"Pine needles!" he shouted. "Get up there!"

What was he talking about?

"Go . . . now! HURRY!"

Why? What did he mean?

Then she saw them—mounds of pine needles riding the water like so much hay. It was crazy! What was happening?

Then, as if a switch had been thrown, the cliffs across the Deep Creek began to stream. Water was coming down in solid sheets, crashing over the rocks, into the river. Waterfalls everywhere! Hundreds of them!

A yell from upstream swung Amy around the other way. A black figure was tumbling in the water like driftwood, flailing and bobbing toward her. Rick! Amy ran straight into the water, grabbing a handful of brush at the edge.

61

The current tore at her legs, but she willed herself to reach him, willed her arm to grow longer, *longer*. He was trying to swim, his arms chopping across the current. Somehow he snagged a footing, lunged. She let go of the brush to meet him. He grabbed the light and his weight swung her around downstream.

"I've got you," she screamed. "Hang on!" He did, and they stumbled back into the shallows, onto the sand, where he collapsed in her arms—shaking and choking. She held him there against her. She kissed his hair, his ear, so glad to have him safe she couldn't speak.

Then Rick was pulling away and the words exploded from his mouth like sobs. "Couldn't get there—God!—It's hopeless!"

Amy drew back in horror. "Ben? He's still in that cave?"

He doubled over with choking. "River's all over in there—no way—"

As Amy's insides collapsed, every scrap of reason disappeared. She grabbed a handful of T-shirt and started yanking him around, crying and hitting. "You left him there? You just left him?"

"Couldn't get there!" He held her away by the wrists. "Nobody could! The trail's gone—eaten up. The river took me. Stop it, Amy, you don't know—*you weren't there!*"

Her breath came in ragged gasps as she fought for control.

Then Steve's arms clamped around her from behind, his chest shaking violently against her back.

"Get her up there," he yelled. "We're out of time!"

6

"When did it start?" Clyde asked in a voice thick with sleep. He raised onto one elbow and peered out of the cave.

"I don't know," Ben shouted. "I just woke up and all this thunder and lightning was goin' on."

Clyde unzipped his bag and sat up. Flashes bright as day showed him what was happening before he ever found the headlamp: It was raining cats and dogs out there. As soon as he heard the roar of the river, he knew they were in trouble.

"Put on your shoes," he ordered. "We're leaving."

"But it's pouring. And it's still dark."

"So?"

Lightning close enough to singe their scalps threw them against their bags again.

"Yikes!" cried Ben.

"This ain't no picnic!"

Ben laughed nervously. "At least we're dry. Bet

they're all gettin' soaked. Suckerrrrrs! They should've slept with us, huh?"

When Clyde looked over, Ben was pawing his bag like a restless dog.

"What's the matter?"

"Can't find my socks. Oh heck, look . . . my bag got wet."

Clyde leaned down and felt around the packs until he found Ben's sneakers—socks stuffed inside—and tossed them over. "Would you hurry it up?"

Light was dancing all around them. He could see the hairs in Ben's eyebrows, could see his own hands shaking as he tried to button his jeans. Thunder like clattering chariots went rolling down the canyon, chased by its own echoes. How had they slept through all the noise?

Wrestling on his shoes, Clyde tried hard to control the shaking that took his whole body. He might be dry, but his belly was having convulsions under his T-shirt—and it wasn't the cold. He was scared. He didn't like the sound of the river or the clanging of those rocks rolling along on the bottom. They sounded hollow. It was unreal!

He glanced at his watch. Two forty-four A.M. Dead of the night. No more sleep, dammit, and today's section of Narrows was the hardest. With deep water, how would they get out? Jeez, he'd be wasted by the time he saw Jason again.

Shivering, he got into the sweatshirt that doubled

as pillow. He zipped his rain shell over that and pulled up the hood, the whole time trying to decide if they should rope together as a precaution or leave their packs. He glanced at Ben, whose mouth was open in a cavernous yawn. *He* could care less.

Clyde's mind raced on to The Forks, to Amy and how worried she'd be, then back again to what they'd need. He'd spotted the rope. What about their wading sticks? Ben had planted them in the wet sand and they'd joked about finding a beanstalk when they woke up.

"Stay here. I'm gonna look around," Clyde shouted.

He ducked out into the storm carrying the headlamp.

He ducked right back. It was like stepping into the shower. Lightning popped like flashbulbs, but he couldn't see a thing in the downpour.

"It's a real cloudburst!" He pulled the hood farther over his face and this time fastened the Velcro.

Out again, he spotted the Deep Creek with the light and saw that the river had claimed half the sand apron in front of the cave and was now snarling around the base of their tree. The sticks were gone. Up close, the Deep Creek was boiling, with muddy bubbles riding the surface.

Dumped on by water shooting off the cliff, Clyde went scuttling under the overhang a second time, then half crawled to a place where he could aim the

66

beam downcanyon at the trail. He searched the brush next to the cliff. His heart stopped. The trail was gone. The whole riverbank was gone! Water filled the channel cliff to cliff.

Frantically, he swung the light across the river. No bank there, either, only box elder saplings in water up to their knees, bending and shaking in the current, looking scared.

"I need a new Band-Aid," came Ben's voice, sing-songing over the noise of the storm. "You got a Band-Aid someplace?"

Clyde moved out to where Ben couldn't see his face. He leaned against the cliff. Panic filled his chest. *We're cut off and he doesn't know. He's worried about a Band-Aid, dear Jesus. What do we do if the storm keeps on, if the river keeps rising?*

And it would, he realized, seeing water fill the suck pools around his feet.

He lunged back away from the rock. Rain hit him full in the face, but he searched the cliff above them for cracks, ledges, plants, irregularities—for *anything*—for any *way* they could pull themselves up to a safer place.

Clyde saw only smooth walls rising hundreds of feet. They even slanted the wrong way.

He covered the cliff opposite where they'd seen a landslide, knowing full well they couldn't cross over. There were waterspouts everywhere—gushing, slackening, starting up again, water dropping a thousand feet off the rim. The plateau must be saturated. It was dumping everything into the canyon, and they were the gophers at the bottom of the hole.

Was there any hope for waiting it out? Clyde tried to judge by the width of the canyon here, which was many yards across, but the river had already swollen twenty times what it was last night.

He continued studying the water, vaguely aware that Ben was still calling. Thunder and lightning were simultaneous now, but the storm was friendly compared to what was happening to the Deep Creek. It would reach them in no time and it would fill the cave. What then? The rocks humping up in the river were monsters. They'd be crushed to death if they weren't drowned. Choose your own ending, he thought sardonically.

The rope! Clyde put the headlamp on over his rain hood and was back at the tree in three strides, wading in water above his ankles. Hurrying, he pulled himself onto the bottom branch, reached up and untied the rope, then went a fork higher so he could spotlight the river from above.

Water everywhere. Both directions. They were trapped. Ben was waiting for him in the only place the river hadn't reached.

Clyde leaned against the tree and felt the thunder reverberate through its trunk. Cold water slid down

68

the rear of his jeans. Why hadn't he stayed at the promontory with the others? Because he was stupid, that's why! After feeling so sorry for Jason . . . Jason was lucky! *He* was the one who was going to die.

Clyde climbed back down with his heart pounding.

He found Ben sitting stiffly against the rear wall of the cave. With his windbreaker zipped up to his chin and his knees drawn close, he occupied a very small space. He wasn't asking for Band-Aids anymore. He knew.

Clyde dropped to the sand and struggled to keep from crying. He was soaked—jeans, socks, his shoulders where the waterproofing failed—and he shook like crazy. "Got any ideas? The trail's gone. We can't get back 'til the river goes down."

"Will it come in here?"

Clyde took off the headlamp, set it so it would spot the base of the box elder.

"I don't know. Judging by that tree, it's rising fast. I think we should—" His mouth turned down of its own accord and he had to stop talking. "I—uh—I think we ought to pack, okay?" He looked the other way and blinked, then got to his knees and scooped up his sleeping bag. "Come on, Ben, punch it! Help me pick up. This place looks like a pigsty."

Panic was making him use his father's voice: "Your room looks like a pigsty! Don't you care that your mother and I provide you with all these nice things?"

Clyde began shoving his sleeping bag into the stuff sack, forcing air out with both fists. Water streaked from his hair into his mouth. Just keep moving, he told himself, trying to swallow. Water everywhere and his throat dry as paper!

Then Ben was tugging on his sleeve. "Hey, would you listen a minute? What's that noise?"

"It's the waterfalls. They're falling all over the place. Free showers, you need one?"

"No, not that. Something else. I *been* hearing it."

Clyde stopped, lifted his head.

"Is it jets?"

Hair stiffened on Clyde's scalp. "Jets—" He looked around at Ben, who stared back like he was paralyzed. "I don't think so."

Whatever it was, it was heading their way. A low rumbling. Not smooth like jets.

Clyde sat back on his heels and strained to tune out everything else. It sounded like a freight train crossing the plains on the Union Pacific line, a night sound he knew from his grandma's farm outside Bartley.

"Hey, Grandma, there were eighty-two cars and two cabooses!"

"Don't tell me you ran down to the pasture and counted them!"

Ben left his pack and crawled over to Clyde, who pulled him in close against his side. Ben didn't seem

70

to care that Clyde was wet and covered with sand, that his legs were doing the sewing machine. With the real killer on its way, it didn't matter about their rat's nest of a cave anymore.

There are four signs of flash flooding, Clyde remembered with solemn clarity.

Who's scared of a flash flood? Jason had said that day. *I'd just catch a board and surfride out of there.* And Jason had jumped up on a curb, knees flexed, arms out, dipping and bobbing like a pro. . . .

Clyde came back. Four signs, the literature said. Three of them already—the rain, the rising water, the muddy color. Number four was the increasing roar of water upcanyon.

And it was getting louder all the time, which meant nearer. A wall of water was bearing down on them and there was no place to go. Suddenly Clyde couldn't get his breath. He was drowning, and in the process he squeezed Ben so tight the boy stiffened and pulled away.

"Don't worry!" cried Ben. "If the cave gets flooded, we'll go up in that tree." He grabbed the light and sent it traveling all the way up the trunk to where the topmost branches whipped around in graceful arcs.

Distracted by fear, all Clyde could think was "It's so beautiful!" Amy's word, *beautiful*. He wished she could see the leaves dancing in the light.

71

Remembering Amy was a shot of adrenalin. *She loves this dumb little kid! I can't just sit here and let us get pulped!*

Simultaneously, some logic about the size of the tree began to register. The trunk—what was it?— five, six inches? The tree was bigger than most they'd seen in the Narrows. That meant it had been there awhile.

"Hold it!" Clyde took the light from Ben and crawled to the mouth of the cave, where he stood and aimed the beam upstream. A stone's toss away, a narrow fin of rock ran down from the cliff and jutted into the river. They could never climb it, but it might be deflecting the water . . . just enough.

A second later Clyde was pushing bags, packs, everything, to the rear of the cave and breathing hard through his mouth. "You got anything else to put on? Gloves, hat?"

"No, but I'm not too freezing."

"You will be." Clyde hauled a red plaid shirt out of Ben's pack, put it over his head like a scarf, tied the sleeves under his chin. Ben made a face, but let him do it. Clyde strapped on the headlamp and grabbed up his rope. "Let's go!"

But Ben had dived back to the gear pile and was tugging out his pack.

"Come on," Clyde yelled, "we don't need that stuff!"

"Wait a sec, my Swiss Army knife! It's brand-new."

"Leave it! We'll be cleaned out like bugs!"

In one furtive move, Ben transferred the knife from a side flap to his jeans pocket, then flung himself after Clyde.

The water between the cave and the tree was up to Ben's knees, with holes even deeper. The rain blinded them, and the water set their feet down where they didn't intend, its force threatening to take Ben every second. At the last, Clyde lifted him to his side with a fierce grip, praying as hard as he ever had.

The ground was throbbing now with the pounding of boulders being carried in the river. Sticks, branches, whole trees bobbed past. In the main channel, Ben saw pine needles riding the swells like after-Christmas sweepings.

Over the roar of the Deep Creek plunging toward confluence came the other roar, so immediate Clyde's mind just quit functioning. The only message reaching his body from his brain was "Up the tree!"

A minute later, they were both high in the tree, with Ben wrapped around the spindly upper trunk like a koala bear. Clyde stood on a middle branch, his face at Ben's chest, his arms around Ben's legs and rear end. He thought of tying them in. No time. The grinding roar had reached the volume of *ten* freight trains.

Then it hit, and the earth rocked with the explosion. An unbelievable mountain of rocks and logs surged past, pushed by a five-foot wall of water that roared by like a nuclear-powered broom. Mud sprayed to the heavens—into their mouths, their eyes. The tree, *everything*, shook helplessly under the barrage.

"I'm dead!" Clyde told himself when the water rose to his waist, then his armpits. He couldn't move. The force of the water pasted him to the tree. On the downside, it was trying just as hard to dislodge Ben.

"Hang on!" Clyde screamed and locked his hands behind Ben.

Trees stripped to logs churned and swirled and thudded against the cliffs and each other, bobbing dangerously close before plunging on. Rocks big as Volkswagens—luminous in the light—humped and clanged as they rolled downstream.

Clyde was hit and full of pain before he knew what had happened. "Hold me!" he screamed.

Arms tightened around his neck, smashing his face and the headlamp against the trunk.

Then everything went black. Quiet came in like a gift. Peace. *I'm drowning. So this is what it's like? It's not so bad. Everything just goes black. I'm not afraid.*

But he wasn't drowning, he was coming back. He was still there hanging on, with the terrifying noise and the cold . . . and a right leg that had gone mercifully numb.

Clyde's reasoning, clear as ever again, told him they couldn't last. The tree dipped and swayed with their weight, and the mega-Jacuzzi pounding his back—he knew!—would also be tearing sand right out from under the roots. But a fierce will to live rose up in him. He couldn't die! *Help me, Mom, help me!* If he died, she'd be alone—he had to live! He pressed his face against the tree and threw all his strength into his arms.

Three of them, crazy to survive—Ben, tree, him!—with his body shielding the tree even as it held them above the flood.

Clyde's brain flashed onto biology class and symbiosis: "Two dissimilar organisms . . . linked in a mutually beneficial relationship."

He prayed for the box elder first.

7

They all sat clumped together—shaking, depressed, no one talking. The cold zeroed right into their bones as the two rivers pounded and raged less than a foot below the mound.

When the tons of debris had exploded out of the Deep Creek an hour ago, Amy had thought it was the end. Now, though sick with grief, she tried to be thankful for what seemed a miracle. Five of them were still alive.

Imagining how it had been for Ben and Clyde made her crazy. The others had tried to help—comforting and holding her when talk was impossible—but the pain was terrible. No one could have lived through such a scouring of that canyon. The rivers were still swollen a hundredfold.

When do you stop missing a younger brother who calls you his "sibling unit"? Do you ever stop missing someone? she wondered. Oh, Ben, I brought you in here! I did this to you! She blinked back the feelings that threatened to swamp her again.

How would she ever tell her parents? Her only brother, their only son. There was no way to tell Ben's friends, either—the twins, Aaron and Annie, or Ian across the street, members of Ben's original Sleeping-Standing-Up-Club.

Attacked again by a spasm of shaking, Amy burrowed into Rick's chest, but it didn't help. His poncho was brittle, the clothes underneath soaked. When he doubled her hand inside his fist, even his palms were clammy. Hurry, sun! Come on, sunrise! We'll all die of exposure!

With daylight coming on, they could at least make out each other's faces, and they all looked like refugees—mud-splattered, hair plastered to their heads or hanging in clumps. Rick's beard had started to grow, which gave him a tense, dark look at the jawline. And though the storm had moved on, the icy gusts of wind and rain kept them on edge.

"Hang in there, kids," Steve shouted across Audrey. "Water's going down on the Deep Creek—I can hear it. Should know something by noon—or maybe sooner."

"Noon!" Amy groaned.

Rick fished for his lighter, held the flame near his wrist. Amy leaned in close to see, as did Neale from the other side. It was 4:28 A.M.

"I want outa here," Neale said thickly, half crying.

"I want my mom. I'm scared. You hear me? I can't stand this!"

"So who can?" Rick yelled back. "We're as stranded as you are."

"Don't give up, kiddo," Steve called. His words came out as stiff as Neale's. "Flash flood's like a tornado. Hit-and-run. Hits hard, goes down fast." He motioned off toward the North Fork, shouting, "That one drains a bigger watershed than the Deep Creek, though. We may be in for more."

More! Amy's mouth tasted like metal, but she reached over and started rubbing Neale's arms and hands.

Steve was right, though she'd tried to ignore the signs. Steadily, eerily almost, as if someone had switched speakers on a stereo, the volume of the North Fork was increasing even as the Deep Creek subsided. But how much more could one little promontory take without just disappearing? The trees below were all gone except one.

Suddenly Neale lunged away from Amy. "I want out. I hate it here!"

"Better get a fire going," Steve shouted over the roar. "Neale's in trouble!"

Her teeth had been clattering out of control for the last hour, but all of a sudden she was acting funny, too. Her speech went haywire, and her arms flew around like a puppet's. Muttering at first, then swearing, she smacked Audrey in the face, shoved Amy a good one in the stomach.

"Stop it!" Amy shoved her back. "What's the matter with you?"

"I'm going home, you A-holes!—I'm sick an' tired . . ."

"She's losing it!" Rick cried at Amy's ear.

Immediately Audrey was on her knees, reaching past Neale, yanking on Rick's poncho. "Is your stove up here?" she shouted.

"Yeah, in my pack."

"Fire it up. She needs something hot."

They all jumped up. Neale, in those few seconds, had struggled to her feet and was zipping out of the wet bag she'd been sitting in.

"Goin' home, gettin' out of here! What'd you do with my mother?" Her voice got higher and faster. "My mother's Louanna Dwyer an' we live on Chestnut an' she's—" Then Amy couldn't understand her at all. She wasn't talking sense, she was babbling.

Hypothermia!

Amy grabbed Neale with both hands to keep her from flying off somewhere. "Is there a dry bag?" she yelled.

Steve had already found one—Amy's, in fact, which wasn't exactly dry. By then Neale was lunging away and Amy had to struggle to keep her from flinging herself over the edge. No wonder she was spacey with cold—she was still barefooted and in shorts!

Steve and Amy wrestled Neale down and inside the bag. She fought the whole time, filling the air with her garbage talk, not making a lick of sense. Amy could hear Rick pumping up the backpacking stove and Audrey stirring drink mix in a pan of water.

The blue flame leaping above the gas jet looked like a ministering angel, and Amy craved warming her hands over it. She'd never been so cold—so frighteningly cold—in her life. Now, with Neale, she understood for the first time what happens when the body temperature plunges into the danger zone. It could happen to any of them.

Amy wrenched off Rick's wet Patagonia jacket and the wet shirt underneath, then forced Neale into the black-and-white wool shirt Steve handed her: his birthday present.

Several minutes later, Amy was holding a Sierra cup to Neale's mouth. The hot cherry punch smelled heavenly and the metal cup warmed her all the way to the elbows and she shivered with unexpected pleasure.

"Take it slow, so you won't get burned," Amy cautioned, but Neale knocked the cup away and slopped punch all over the bag.

"Neale! Come on, you have to!"

Once Neale got a taste, she gulped the rest in

seconds, with Amy hoping she wasn't burning her mouth.

Audrey was right there at her elbow pouring seconds and thirds, telling Amy to take a swallow herself. "I did," she said, "right out of the pan."

In the meantime, Rick had pulled out their stash of granola bars and was handing them around. "You, too, Amy," he yelled over the roar.

No way could she choke down food! But she knew Neale needed carbohydrates *fast* after eating so little the night before—a dab of spaghetti and some carrot sticks. People died of hypothermia all the time according to the sports magazines.

Dunking one bar, then the other, Amy coaxed and scolded until Neale finished two.

Audrey, being the smallest, had changed into a dry shirt and slacks, then quickly came over and squeezed into the sleeping bag with Neale. Amy zipped them up, pulled the hood around their heads.

The three of them then passed the pan around— Steve and Rick and Amy—and drank what was left. Amy held the sweet red Wyler's in her mouth a long time before letting it slide down her throat. The pure comfort of it made her think of home, and as her eyes filled, she had to look away.

"Everything okay?" Amy asked a bit later, bending over the double hump in the sleeping bag.

Audrey mouthed, "Thanks."

81

Amy envied them. They'd soon be warm and toasty in her North Face bag. *Her* bag, that went down to minus ten. It was all she had left. Her backpack, dropped during the first scramble up the mound and forgotten, was long gone. The extra clothes, the camera, the great pictures . . .

She wondered if her pack would make it all the way to the Temple of Sinawava, where the Virgin River came out above the Visitor's Center.

Look, tourists would say, *someone's pack. How odd!*

Not likely. It would end up buried in the mud somewhere.

Cruelly, the image twisted and her pack became Ben and all the grief returned with a flood of tears. This time she couldn't stop.

"Amy, don't! You have to keep hoping—you can't give up," Rick said, pulling her close. But she stiffened and turned away from him.

What was wrong? She had to stop blaming Rick. Did she think she'd have made it to the cave? Somehow made it, even though he couldn't?

She twisted around so her back was against him and put her hands over her ears—as if muffling the incessant roar would also stop the thinking.

The next hour passed more slowly than the Jurassic Age.

Every few seconds a shudder tore through Amy's body. It had been easier rushing around taking care of Neale. Now everyone was jumpy again, their fears building right along with the North Fork.

Using gas from Steve's backpacking stove, the men had got a small fire going and were feeding it with wood Audrey and Steve had collected the day before. They built it as close to Neale as they dared, then hunkered over it, warming themselves and drying out.

Neale was now sitting up in the bag, eating cheese and drinking tea. The others had agreed to begin rationing what they had left, so they were doing without.

Audrey was up and moving, checking supplies, tying knots in the plastic bags, keeping busy. When Steve waded down to the tree to tie in his rope, Amy had the fire to herself and crept closer. It wasn't a big fire, but it was a lifesaver. It also allowed them to see the edges that had broken off when the Deep Creek crested. Their grassy mound now looked like corduroy, with big creases everywhere.

Sitting with her arms around her knees, Amy thought of the great blazing fires her dad made on their fall trips to the mountains. He'd set up his sooty black pot, throw in a cut-up chicken, potatoes, carrots, onions, a ton of pepper. He'd make up a dumb song about his soup—always a different song—

which he sang tunelessly at the top of his lungs to make Ben and her laugh.

Suddenly the yearning to be on Diamond Mountain was overwhelming. She wanted to be tearing over the trails on a mountain bike, the three of them hollering, dipping into gullys, stopping in the high clearings to laugh and drink in the yellow aspen, so bright the color burned holes in the evergreen landscape.

"I can't make it this year," she'd told her dad just last Sunday. "The wedding will take six weeks easy! I don't have enough days left."

He'd looked so disappointed. What shortage of days had she been talking about? She didn't know what it was to be out of days!

The fire blurred as Amy saw BENJAMIN RIRELY—1933 through her tears, and saw again the aspen where old Ben Rirely had carved his name. The letters were hard to read, having been stretched and pulled by the growing tree.

"You were named after that old sheepherder," her dad told Ben when he was little. Teasing, of course.

Ben! Oh please, God—

Then Rick had hold of her arm and was pulling her to her feet. "Come on, get up here with the rest of us. It's coming!"

Sure enough, the ground was starting to vibrate. The North Fork was about to blow. She wanted to stay by the fire, to pretend everything was all right, to have Ben back and everything like it was . . .

Neale stood between Steve and Audrey, one hand clutching the sleeping bag to her waist. Her face looked gaunt in the early light and Amy felt sorry for her. She felt sorry for them all.

Steve's hands shook as he passed the looped end of the rope to Amy and motioned for her to send it along to Rick. Why do we need a rope this time?

The roar was terrible now.

"BOTH HANDS!" Steve lifted both hands to show them. "DON'T LET GO, NO MATTER WHAT!"

Amy's heart banged against her ribs. Another wall of water! How could it be happening? The little stream they'd practically invented at Chamberlain's Ranch . . .

"Here it comes!" screamed Neale, ducking her head.

Amy grasped the rope with one hand, Rick with the other, and pushed into the cliff with all her might.

The ground heaved. The plug broke out of the narrow canyon with the power of a volcanic eruption. Twenty-, thirty-foot logs shot through the scant opening like darts from a gun, to go caroming off the opposite cliff. The noise battered their bodies, their ears. Rocks, logs, mud—shot past them into the confluence, pushed by a wall of water so towering Amy leaped when she saw it.

85

Dear God, three times higher than the Deep Creek!
Instantly the area filled with churning flood-waters.

Amy gasped as a red tongue swept away their fire. She screamed when a chunk of land broke off, toppling Rick's pack and forcing him to leap away.

The list he'd made, the one she'd never found, was suddenly emblazoned on her brain. "Food, lotion, clothes . . ." All twelve items. Stupid list! Everything gone and now us!

Seconds more and the water was over their feet.

8

"What time is it?" came Ben's tired voice. "How long we been here?"

"Six hours . . . eight. Don't know. My watch quit, remember?"

Clyde leaned away from the tree and studied the gray dogleg of sky that showed overhead. The clouds were dark—full-bellied—making it hard to judge time, but his stomach had been growling over an hour.

"Must be ten by now," he answered.

No matter. An hour hanging in the tree was an eternity. He'd aged a hundred years during one night.

The tree had aged, too, and leaned pitifully toward the confluence—a battered senior citizen like himself. There was now a permanent high-water mark on the trunk, a raw place that had been dug into the bark from Clyde's jeans button, from holding the two of them to the swaying box elder through the worst of it.

Now Clyde let go of the tree one hand at a time to work his stiff fingers. He hunched his shoulders, which hurt even more than his hands, then pounded on his bony rear end that was numb from leaning on the pipe-stem branches.

"We can't stay cramped here forever," he shouted. "The cave's almost clear. Be lots better if we could get over there."

Ben still clung near his original perch, too cold or too scared to move.

Clyde worked his way down the tree as he'd done several times before, but this time he plunged a foot in the water. The shock sucked up his stomach. It was like ice! He made himself do it again, sliding his right foot down the trunk, gasping as he searched for the bottom branch. No luck. He changed feet, checked the other side of the tree.

"Oh my heck!" he muttered. There were only stubs. The lower branches had been sheared right off. He'd come *that* close.

The water was freezing, but he forced himself to put full weight on the stub to see how much he could stand. Watching the liquid mud part thickly around his leg, Clyde realized that the temperature more than the current would keep them in the tree awhile longer, something he hadn't thought of before.

Clyde pulled up to where he could swing his injured leg free. The knee was tender and swelling all the way around, but he couldn't tell what kind of handicap it would be. There was no longer blood running down the back of his leg, which made him think the wound must have closed.

He measured the distance that separated them from the cave. With the water going down, things looked hopeful, but the current was still plenty treacherous. It would be impossible for Ben. Maybe it was impossible for him.

He wondered if they could make it through another night without a fire or dry clothes. The roar of the Deep Creek coming up in his ears was the answer. If it rained, or if it flooded again, they were goners!

Clyde climbed back up near Ben. "Come on, mate," he shouted, forcing the cheer. "Look alive! We just came through hell and high water together, you know that?"

Ben didn't answer, but stared at the Deep Creek as if mesmerized. He hung on with dead-white knuckles, one leg under him, one dangling.

"Are you okay?" Clyde asked. Ben's shivering periodically gave the whole tree top a fit. "Want to come down by me?"

"I'm—staying—here." Ben's words came out separately.

"Clyde?" he called a minute later.

"Yeah."

"Do you think . . . you think Amy's dead? And the rest . . ."

Clyde winced. "Dead! Oh, gosh, no. You can't think that." He pulled himself another fork closer, wrapped his arms around Ben's legs and held him awhile. *And why not? Haven't you?*

It had been so awful! He'd never be that close to death again, not until it was the real thing. A person knew something like that for sure.

"You know what?" Clyde said, leaning back so he could see Ben's face. "They were probably lots better off on that high place than we were here."

Ben's head went back for a sneeze, then two more. Unthinking, he wiped his nose on Clyde's shoulder, but Clyde pretended he didn't see.

"But"—Ben wasn't finished—"what if they didn't wake up in time? We almost didn't. What if the river just boiled in there—"

"The rain would wake them up. They were sleeping under the stars, not like us. What's funny is— I bet they're talking about us right now, same as we're talking about them. Amy's saying, 'Oh, poor Ben, poor Ben!' And here you are, mean as ever."

Momentarily, Ben's eyes lit up, but he was still thinking the worst.

Clyde finally got Ben to smile by grabbing hold of his knobby knee and shifting it through the gears, making authentic Ferrari sounds. Jason sometimes got his dad's Ferrari.

"Listen up, kid, I got a riddle for you. What's wet and cold and muddy all over?" Clyde consulted his dead watch. "You got ten seconds. Tick—tick—tick—tick—"

"Me?"

"Verrrry good! I'm impressed. You must eat Wheaties."

"Amy does. I eat junk food."

"One more." Clyde swung to the other side of the trunk. "What's wet and cold and red-headed . . . and obscenely good-looking?"

Grudgingly Ben smiled again. "I suppose you mean yourself."

Clyde shook his head in amazement. "I can't get over it. A gifted child! Where did you say you went to kindergarten?"

Clyde felt Ben's sneaker searching for a footing, so he raised up his knee to make a shelf, saying, "What are friends for? Go ahead, put your weight on it. I like being walked on better than anything else."

Ben chuckled. "I know a real riddle if I can think of it." He stared off a minute, chewed on his lip.

"Ten seconds," Clyde said. "Tick—tick—tick—"

"No, wait. Okay, okay, I got it. How do you spell spot?"

"Easy. S-p-o-t."

"Now spell what you do on a green light."

"S-t-o-p."

Ben doubled over laughing. "Gol, don't drive me anywhere!"

Clyde grinned and knuckled Ben in the ribs when he caught on. "Hey, bro, I'm gonna get you for that."

"Oh, ow!" Ben yelled suddenly. "I got a charley horse!"

"Oh no! Don't get a cramp on me! Where is it?"

Ben pounded the leg that was still doubled under him. "Owwwww, what do I do? It's killing me!"

"Pull up so you can straighten it out."

"Can't!" Ben's face screwed up. "Hurts too much!"

Clyde got both hands around Ben's sneaker trying to pry it out. "Come on, you have to help me. Take your weight off or I can't get it."

Ben was panting, half crying, but Clyde finally wrenched the foot out of the crotch of the tree.

"Come on, Charley!" he yelled, working the muscles with both hands.

"Keep goin'," Ben cried. "Oh, man, it's murder, I can't stand it!"

Ben's skin was pure clammy. A cramp would be the least of their problems if the sun didn't hurry and show. They had to get out, get some help. They were *survivors*; they couldn't die of exposure!

Clyde went on rolling and kneading Ben's pitifully small muscles. For once, he wished for extra fat.

Gobs of fat! Lightweights like Ben and him, they didn't have an extra ounce anywhere.

Once he got Ben to a lower branch, Clyde made him do exercises. Ben had tears at first, but he finally warmed up enough to swing an arm, then a leg. Grabbing hands, they did pushpulls back and forth, back and forth. They disco'd in the air, they marched. Finally they sang, "Oh, say can you seeeee any bedbugs on meeeee . . ."

Clyde could feel the old optimism coming back with the circulation.

When he accidentally ended up with a tuft of spiky hair, Ben turned spastic with pointing and giggles. Soon they were egging each other on with wild hair-dos—muddy Mohawks and Elvis Presleys. The more they laughed, the better it felt.

Clowning around, Clyde could hear his dad say, *that's all you're good for!*

When water blew down on them from a cliff all of a sudden, they sobered in a hurry. Clyde held his breath to see if it really was raining.

"What are we laughing about?" he said grimly.

"I don't know," Ben whispered.

It was hard work cutting through green branches with a Swiss Army knife.

"Poor tree," Ben had muttered, patting its trunk while Clyde sawed away. "You're gonna be really lopsided now. But we want to live, too."

Clyde had smiled listening to him. It was true. They'd become attached to the tree emotionally as well as physically.

After what seemed like an hour of hacking and trimming, it was Ben's job to hang on to the walking sticks while Clyde tied one end of his rope to the trunk, the other around his waist. The headlamp, zipped inside the pouch of his rain jacket since daylight, he strapped back on so it was less likely to get wet.

"Knife, rope, headlamp." He named over their possessions.

Clyde thought of Clue, the parlor game he and Jason had played for hours when they were little. Make the headlamp a candlestick, all they lacked was a wrench and a gun, neither of which would do them any good. A set of dice? Yeah, they could sure use the dice.

"Okay," Clyde said, giving another tug to the square knot at his waist. "Give me that big stick. I'm going in."

He slid one foot along the trunk to the stump. "Oh Jeez, I must be crazy!" The noise of the Deep Creek down close made everything scarier, and suddenly it was hard to breathe.

"Wait!" Ben grabbed his arm. "What if—what do I do if—"

"Keep your fingers crossed!" Clyde shouted, wishing he felt as brave as he sounded.

He let go, dropped. His shivers turned to convulsions. The water wasn't quite up to his jockeys, thank God. Cold like that could take care of a guy's manhood for all time.

Standing on the bottom, he was in above his knees and dealing with a current that was still plenty wicked. The water had warmed a few degrees, but no one in his right mind would swim in it.

He stood there a minute, shaking and clinging to the tree, thinking he should say something more to Ben. They mightn't be able to hear each other later.

"Stay put! If it's too bad, you may have to wait. So hang on good, you understand?"

Ben's forehead bunched up.

"You all right?" Clyde reached up and poked him with the walking stick, which Ben pushed back with a tough smile.

Then, getting up his nerve, Clyde took one step away from the tree, still holding on, but wanting to test the current. It pummeled the backs of his legs and the pain spiraled right up his thigh. "Wrong way!" he muttered.

He pulled back to the tree again, changed hands, pivoted to face upstream. His knee still gave him fits, but he figured he'd be okay if he could just stay low. He dug the pole into the mud and hunched over it. Okay, better! It's better facing the current.

Moving sideways—a wounded crab—he kept the rope taut and mucked along six inches at a time, breathing loud and hard. The water coming at him made him dizzy, so he had to look up, look off.

"Keep going!" Ben shouted. "You're doin' great!"

Clyde grinned. He was! He actually was. A new bottom had been laid down by the flood, and although his feet sank in with every step, the mud was easier than the slick rocks he'd been expecting.

The last steps to the sandbar were a cinch; then Clyde was the one who felt like crying.

"I made it!" he yelled to Ben, big blobs coming up in his eyes. He scooped up a handful of sloppy sand and threw it at the cliff. Reenacting Columbus, for hell's sake!

Ben, who was bouncing up and down in the tree, gave him a thumbs-up sign. Crazy kid! Clyde wished he had his camera. The red plaid shirt tied around Ben's neck was the one bright spot in the whole ravaged canyon.

Clyde signaled "in a minute" to Ben, then dropped down onto the sand and stretched out. He was shaking with cold, but he closed his eyes and sucked in deep breaths of canyon air that suddenly smelled wonderful and fresh. He hurt everywhere—hips, knees, ankles, back, his throat that was parched for a drink. Every muscle, every joint. His stomach was in knots. If he could just fall asleep and not wake up 'til it was over!

You try it, Jason! Try hanging in a tree that long.

Clyde's eyes had been burning for hours from irritants and lack of sleep, but now, suddenly, his eyelids were flooded with a searing orangey red that could only mean the sun. He opened his eyes. Dear Jesus, the warmth of that sun.

He held his breath watching the wall opposite light up, seeing all the colors heighten as if by magic. Thank God, the sun!

He motioned for Ben to turn around and see the cliffs.

For the first time, getting out of the Narrows alive seemed a real possibility. If the river kept dropping, they might make it back to The Forks by noon. The current would be with them, at least, and they could hug the cliff. It wouldn't be like fighting their way upstream.

With Ben shouting his excitement from the tree, Clyde got to his feet, looped the rope into his hand and gripped the walking stick. His knee throbbed and his clinging jeans made him shake with cold, but now he had hope.

"Here goes nothin'!" he hollered back. He set his jaw and waded in—more confident, but respectful still of a current that showed no favors.

He'd get Ben across first. Then he'd go back and untie the rope. After that . . .

Don't plan too far ahead. You don't know what you'll find at the confluence.

Like some of the best stories he'd ever told, he'd have to make this one up as he went along.

9

When the sun broke through the clouds just before noon, it was everyone else who did the cheering, not Amy.

Neale spread her arms and attempted a Snoopy twirl, looking a little like Charlie Chaplin in Steve's extra pair of pants. It was her first big smile of the weekend, so far as Amy knew.

"Two good things!" Neale shouted, shaking victory signs over her head. "Water's going down . . . the sun's out."

"Three," Rick corrected her. "We lived through it. That's the best news."

Amy spun around and glared at him.

"I mean"—his hands went up—"all of *us* are alive. And think about it a minute. We were eyewitnesses to two really awesome flash floods, and we're here to tell about it."

His voice trailed off when Amy turned back to the Deep Creek where she was collecting driftwood. She cast out the tree limb she was fishing with. It sang on the surface, then throbbed when she forced it into the current.

How could he be so insensitive? she wondered. Talking about the most horrible nightmare as if it were some kind of opportunity! Neale was just as bad. All of them! How could they be so stupidly happy to see the sun, when Ben, when Clyde . . .

She looked off up the canyon, to the rockslide where the river curved out of sight, noticing again how there wasn't a hint of green anywhere. The sunlight showed bare-naked cliffs. Oh Ben!

She dropped the branch and clutched her arms over her chest. She felt as if someone had scored her insides with a sharp blade, then left her draining away. The noise, too, was driving her crazy. Would it never let up, that stupid, persistent roar? It wore her down, turned everything anyone did or said into a stupid irritation. Rick especially grated on her. How could she marry someone who got on her nerves so much?

"Come stand in the sun," Audrey called. "It can't last, you know, not with so many clouds."

Amy kicked the fishing stick onto the pile and dried her hands on her jeans. She hesitated, staring at the Deep Creek another minute, thinking that

100

there wouldn't be a wedding, anyway, if Ben was dead. She forced herself to join the others.

Audrey, Steve, Neale, now Rick, stood along the edge of the shrunken mound, faces up to catch the sun. Steve was so tall he looked tippy until he put his hands on Audrey's shoulders.

"How much we need sunlight!" Audrey was saying. "I feel like a crocus that's been waiting for the sun all winter."

Funny lady! She kept surprising Amy, who had never known anyone so eager to give everything away and make do for herself. Even now Audrey was the one moving over, pulling Steve along so there'd be room.

"Come on in here," Steve tugged at Amy's sleeve. "You have to take advantage."

So they stood clumped together like sun-worshipers, scarcely talking, soaking up rays. As the warmth penetrated her skin, Amy felt herself start to relax.

"Nice, huh?" Neale nudged her.

Amy sighed. "Like understanding photosynthesis for the first time."

A minute later, Amy reached for Rick's hand and forgave him for being glad to be alive. She couldn't force a smile, but in scrutinizing his face she saw how haggard he looked. His fingers were jumpy and cold, too, which wasn't usual.

What made her so selfish? She wasn't the only one who had suffered. Why couldn't she be as hopeful as the others? Maybe the tree at the cave *had* saved the boys. Steve insisted it was sturdy. Amy studied the cottonwood on the tier below, whose branches were now clotheslines for sleeping bags and Audrey's jeans. The tree looked violated, its bare roots exposed—from water going under as well as around it.

But it's standing, Amy told herself, it's still standing.

Suddenly, her hopes broke through right along with Audrey's crocus and she turned around to face Steve. "How soon can we go up there?"

"*I* wouldn't get in that river yet," Rick said, scowling. "Not me!"

Steve walked slowly over to creekside. The two of them followed, Rick nervously running his hands in and out of his rear pockets, saying, "It's deceptive, that's the trouble. A current's always worse than it looks."

"What do you think?" Amy asked Steve.

Rick picked up a piece of wood, chucked it at the pile.

"Well, we're a lot closer than we were an hour ago." Steve stroked his mustache, studying the river in both directions. "I'd be willing to test it here pretty soon, but I'd want to be on a line to try it out." He looked around. "Once we start up there, it better be two of us in case of injuries."

They'd discovered that morning that Steve knew a thing or two about risks. He was an engineer who'd installed everything from ski lifts to pipelines. He was a hiker and rock climber when he had the chance. In his day, as he put it, he'd gone up cracks and chimneys as vertical as many they'd seen in the Narrows. "But only with equipment," he'd added.

Rick stood there, nodding but not talking.

"There are some things to do first," Steve said. Then to Amy, with a pat on her shoulder. "I know you're beside yourself."

The morning had been the longest and saddest of her life, that's all.

"We'll need good strong walking sticks," he went on, so Neale and Audrey came over and they all went through the driftwood. They found several that had been tumbled smooth, and Neale gave one of them to Rick.

He tested it across his knee, then dug it into the mound. Amy watched as he stomped around trying it out. He kept looking up the Deep Creek, then off down the canyon where the water was still plenty nasty. He also kept licking his lips. He's scared, she thought. He's thinking about what happened.

"Audrey, where's the first aid?" Steve asked. "Better have a dry sleeping bag, too, hadn't we?"

Audrey pulled Rick's bag out of the plastic storage and shoved it into a daypack without bothering to ask whose it was.

"My luck!" Rick said, down low, to Amy. "There it goes."

"So?" Amy bristled. "You act like . . . What's wrong with you?"

"I'll tell you what's wrong with me. Getting in that river *this soon* is the dumbest thing we've done yet."

"Steve's doing it. If he thinks—"

"Yeah—well—Steve and who else?" Rick poked his chest. "Me!"

Neale, who'd been listening to them fight, walked off muttering, "You couldn't get me in that water, not for anything."

Amy glared at her back. "Well, let me tell you, kid, sooner or later you'll have to. But nobody's asking a fourteen-year-old. What do you weigh, anyhow, ninety-eight pounds? Get serious!"

Neale swung around and stuck out her tongue at Amy.

"Lay off her once, would you?" Rick growled. He threw off his poncho, then rolled up his sleeves with quick, jerky movements. So now he was mad as well as scared! Well, who wasn't? She was scared to death there wouldn't be any sign of her brother up that canyon.

Steve didn't pay any attention to the snarling. He calmly stepped into the rope harness he'd made and tied it at the waist. He buckled on the daypack, telling Audrey they'd need a fire when they came in, whether they found the kids or not. His matter-of-fact words were chilling.

"I'm glad someone's got guts around here," Rick told him.

"I wouldn't do it if I didn't think I could." Steve handed the coil to Rick. "I might not need the rope, but—"

Then, as if it was an afterthought, he stepped back, pulled Audrey over, and kissed her on top of the head. "Keep the kids in line," he said wryly, and left her grinning.

Steve raised an arm as he slid down the few feet to the edge of the water. He seemed happy to be doing something, Amy decided. She didn't think it mattered what. They all stood watching, Audrey looking nervous with both hands on her cheeks.

The water was deeper than Amy expected. Steve was in halfway to his crotch on the second step. "Like ice!" he yelled back, but he hugged the cliff and crept on, moving in slow motion—bending forward over the stick, pulling up a foot, then having to wait on the other.

"He's making it!" Amy shouted. "It can't be too bad."

The color was gone from Rick's face when she looked at him next. He was gray as mud, but he kept his eyes on Steve and continued handing out rope, lifting his arms now and again when the rope went slack. She ran her hand down his back, but he stiffened, stepped away.

"Are you okay?" she asked. "Want me to do that?"

"Hell, no!" Then, surprising her with a quick move, he grabbed her by the neck and pushed the rope into her skin. "Feel that? You think that's not some current? He's crazy! There'll be more dead."

Amy twisted away, her eyes burning. She wanted to hit him, but suddenly Audrey had hold of her arm and was leading her past Neale to the North Fork side.

"He's terrified," Audrey said. "You mustn't get mad. And Steve's just an animal when it comes to anything dangerous. You better know that, too."

Amy rubbed her neck where she could still feel the rope and nodded. No way was she going to cry over another of Rick's dumb stunts. "I'm okay," she told Audrey, but she wasn't. She wasn't at all.

They stayed arm in arm, watching, but not talking, as Amy fought back a throatful of feelings.

"Will you believe me now?" Rick called over his shoulder. He pointed to Steve, who had stopped, who was grabbing his breath and resting. He was apparently turning to come back. A minute later, though, he was pointing with his stick and shouting for them to see something in the river. "There! What is it?"

Amy shaded her eyes and searched where he pointed. Suddenly she was screaming and rushing to the edge. "Noooooooo, Ben!"

A flash of red, the plaid she'd seen in his pack! She held her head, straining to see. The spot of red bobbed lifelessly, turned when the current of the North Fork hit it—disappeared—popped up again. Was it Ben? An arm around a log? She screamed again when it swirled out of sight.

Without thought she was in the Deep Creek, pulling herself out to Steve. "Was it Ben?" she cried. Ben tied to a log? Dear God, what was it?

Steve shouted for her to wait. She let the rope go and fell against the rock, dizzy from the water. Her mouth was wide open and she was crying out of control. She heard Rick yelling for her to come back, but all she knew was Ben in that river.

It took both Rick and Steve to get her up the mound, where she fell into Audrey's arms.

"It's okay to cry, it's okay"—Audrey rocked her back and forth—"go ahead, you've had way too much."

"You guys, it wasn't Ben!" Neale insisted. "I tell you, I had a good look and it wasn't Ben."

"What happened?" Rick shouted. "What's going on?"

107

"I spotted it even before Steve," Neale kept on, "and it wasn't a person, Amy, honest." She had Amy's hand, was trying to get her attention. "It was just— I don't know, but it wasn't a body—"

Then Audrey was steering her over to sit on the storage bags, was rubbing her hands while shouting for someone to start a fire. Amy heard Steve unclip his daypack. "I don't know what I saw out there, that's the truth," he told Rick, "but we could make it up there, I'm pretty sure, if you're not afraid of trying. It's not bad."

Then Neale startled everyone with a high-pitched scream. "Look! It's Clyde. Over there, he's alive!"

Amy leaped to her feet, was at the Deep Creek in seconds. *Clyde! Alone!* Her heart was pumping pure adrenalin, but she couldn't make a sound. Steve was there in a second, his hands cupped around his mouth, shouting, "BENNNNNN. IS BEN OKAY?"

Clyde nodded. Hard. He was up out of the water, was standing on a rock there at the bend and was pointing vigorously behind him, to some out-of-sight place, nodding with the whole top half of his body. "He's okaaaaay" came back to them. "Can you come?" The voice sounded miles away, but it reached them from less than twenty yards upstream.

"Let's go!" shouted Steve, hooking the rope to his belt.

Amy didn't wait to be asked. She grabbed a walking stick, threw a stern look at Rick that said, "Don't stop me," and plunged in. Steve, just ahead, reached back for her hand. She dug in her pole and pulled her legs through the current, oblivious to the cold, to the weakness in her knees, to the tears streaming down her face.

"He's alive! He's alive!" she said again and again.

10

"Ben!" Amy shouted, waving like a crazy woman.

Clyde felt like breaking into song himself to see everyone so happy—Amy yelling, Steve shaking a fist overhead.

Poor Ben, looking very small wedged into the rock crevice where he'd left him hip deep in water, appeared to be all eyes and chalky face. He couldn't wave back, but his mouth started going as soon as he saw Amy.

Once Steve came abreast of him in the river, Clyde eased into the water again, dug in his pole, tensed to buck the current. He couldn't stop smiling. It was a whole new ball game knowing everyone was alive.

"Is he hurt?" Steve shouted in his face.

"No, it's too deep for him. Bottom falls right out. Can we ferry him across?"

Suddenly, from the other side, Amy nearly toppled him with a hug. He swung around to find her beaming up at him out of the next-to-dirtiest face he'd seen in the Narrows.

"All *right!*" He laughed. He'd have stood there celebrating all day except for Steve hollering, "Save it, the kid's freezing."

They pulled together for a conference as Steve shouted out a plan, all of them shaking, but looking beyond to where Ben waited for help.

Soon they had Amy up on the rocks where Clyde had been only minutes before. Steve got her into his harness, showed her what to do if there was sudden tension on the rope. She was to be the anchor.

While Steve tied their two ropes together with a fisherman's knot, Amy yelled in Clyde's ear how she'd recognized Ben's shirt going by.

"Oh no!" His stomach lurched knowing what she'd thought. He gestured waving a flag. "We needed a signal . . . case my voice didn't carry. Whole thing got away on the deep stretch." Talking was impossible, but he knew exactly what she meant when she put her hand on her heart.

By the time Steve and he struck out with their probes, Amy was braced and feeding out line. Her face was grim with responsibility, but Clyde figured she and Ben were the happiest people in the state of Utah right then.

*   *   *

The smell of hot chocolate reached them as soon as they came back around the rocks with Ben in tow. They could also smell smoke, see flames. Clyde counted three figures moving around the high ledge, throwing wood on the fire.

SEVEN SURVIVED! He wanted to believe it, but he was a little too superstitious to be making up headlines yet.

Approaching a second time, Clyde could take in what he was seeing. The promontory of land he'd been dreaming about since three A.M. was nothing now but a dirt hill against the cliff. One fair-sized cottonwood remained, a comical sight with all that was draped over it. No lacy greenery. No brushy undergrowth. Here and there a stripped sapling, shaking in the current. The place had been so beautiful—like an island, almost, with its trees and sand.

Clyde limped along with a staff in each hand, favoring his knee, but caring about nothing so much as getting there. He wished he were wearing his "Go With the Flow" T-shirt, because that's how he felt: like a piece of smiling flotsam being carried along by the river. Six beers might have had the same effect.

Ben, too—miserable as he was—suddenly acted as if the whole thing had been a lark. With a wild

112

whoop, he let his legs go floating up between Amy and Steve, who were having a hard enough time hanging onto him. He quit in a hurry when Amy yelled, "Stop that!"

Arriving back where it was safe—for a while, at least—and close enough to see the others' faces, Clyde fought a terrible urge to break down and cry. Again and again he swallowed. It didn't help that Audrey's expression mirrored the way he felt.

"I'm hungry enough to eat bear!" he growled to keep from crying, and came up dripping wet out of the Deep Creek. Everyone else laughed, too.

How great to laugh, to be alive to laugh again!

Rick waded right in to meet them, lifting and hugging Ben, then trying to give everyone a hand up the slope at once. Rick and Amy fell into each other's arms, with Amy swiping at her cheeks and sniffling. Steve apparently got emotional watching *them*. He reached for Clyde on one side, Ben on the other, squeezed and held them tight.

Audrey's welcome, a variation on the Heimlich maneuver, nearly destroyed Clyde's rib cage. "Did you ever pray so hard in your life?" she kept saying.

Even Neale's eyes were swimming. "What'd you guys *do*?" she had to know. "Where'd you go?"

"We were up a tree the whole time!" Ben cried. "Hours and hours! And Clyde got his leg mashed and I had to hang on to him when he blacked out."

"Ben saved us a couple of times," Clyde said when he got a chance. "Man, I lost it! I really panicked with all that water . . . and us trapped in that cave, you know? Then we started hearing those jets coming down the canyon—" Clyde looked away, grabbed a breath. "Old Ben there, he just shines the light up that box elder and says, 'That's where I'm going.' "

"Yeah, I did!"

"Honest, Ben?" Amy grabbed him. "I'm so proud of you. Really, did you hold Clyde up in that tree by yourself?"

"Yep!" He beamed, even as he shivered. "He held me, too, but mostly I was holding him—when he slumped and stuff."

"I thought it was all over," Clyde said. "I was ready to give up, thought we were drowning."

"But I wouldn't let you, would I?"

They all stood around, imitating Ben with their grins, as he went on telling how smart it was to have saved his Swiss Army knife—he pulled the red knife out to show them—but how bad it was that the packs were lost. Besides his pack and camera, he'd lost his new nylon wallet with $6.00. "That's two lawn jobs," he said mournfully.

Amy tugged him closer to the fire. "Come on, Ben, you can change while you talk," she said like an older sister.

"What'd I tell you guys?" Steve rocked back on

114

his heels and looked smug. "Those are two smart kids."

"Hey, Amy," Ben said suddenly. "You know that sleeping bag we borrowed from Ian?" His hands shook hopelessly trying to unzip his windbreaker. "It's gone, too!"

"Oh Ben, who cares? Lots of things are gone."

"Yeah, but what's Ian gonna say?"

"We'll buy him a new one." Amy bent to help with the zipper. "Come on, you'll catch pneumonia."

Audrey, stirring hot chocolate in the coffeepot as she talked, asked if they knew there'd been a second crest on the North Fork. "About daybreak."

"That was the real show!" said Rick. Then the five of *them* were talking over each other, telling how horrible it had been.

Ben yanked off his jacket. "Two walls of water?" he shouted.

Clyde couldn't believe it either: "Worse than the Deep Creek?"

"Oh, much worse!" from Neale and Amy at the same time.

"And it went on for hours—"

"—spewing out one logjam after another."

"Water rose ten, fifteen feet—*in seconds!*" said Steve. "Great big old logs—thirty-footers—shot out of there like jackstraws, ricocheted off that cliff." He pointed opposite. "It was a sight!"

115

"Didn't you hear it?" Rick asked. "The noise must have reached a thousand decibels in here."

While everyone talked, Ben matter-of-factly sat down and tugged on the socks that stuck to him like a second skin. He was now wearing a big shirt Steve had warmed for him, but was taking his time examining blisters and separating his toes with shaky fingers.

"Here," Amy urged, "let me pull off those jeans."

"Nooooo!"

Clyde grinned and turned his back to Ben. At that age, he knew, a guy lives in mortal terror of being seen in his underwear.

Then, as if to show Ben how it was done, wilderness style, Audrey whipped off her tan fatigues right there in plain sight, tossed them to Ben and told him to put them on.

"They won't fit for another thirty years," she said with an offhand wave, "but they're dry. Clean, too, considering. Go on. I have jeans down there on the tree."

Ben looked at his sister and screwed up his face. He didn't actually sneer, or say, "Girl's pants"—but Amy had to poke him twice before he'd unzip.

By then Rick had thrown the ground cloth and a sleeping bag near the fire, so they soon had Ben inside, with Amy arranging things so he could sit up. Audrey handed him a cup of chocolate. "Made with the last canteen water. The next batch won't taste nearly this good."

Ben's teeth clicked on the cup, but he got out a smile and a "Thanks!"

"You're next, Clyde," Audrey called out.

"You wouldn't!" he gasped, clutching his pants.

Rick and Amy laughed, but Audrey pinned him with a squinty look. "You want a cup of this el primo chocolate, or are you gonna stand there and be a smart ass?"

He grinned. "I'd rather have the chocolate than be what you said."

Jason would have been rolling on the ground by now. Snappy-eyed Audrey was a sight in her L. L. Bean shirttails and pink underpants, serving up chocolate like nothing was missing.

Steve had already sloshed into the water to retrieve her jeans. "That outfit you're wearing would look pitiful on anyone else," he said gallantly.

After the hot chocolate, Audrey insisted on mothering Clyde some more, this time by using half her Neosporin on the puncture wound behind his knee.

"Hey, lady, take it easy!" he cried when she tried to clean it out a little. He finally had to bite down on his fist.

"It's not a pretty sight," Audrey said as she wrapped it up with gauze. "I don't know how you'll keep out the infection."

*   *   *

Sunday brunch, as they were calling it, was black
bread and half-cooked bacon, and so little of each
everyone finished hungry. But no one complained.
The wonderfully salty bacon was like manna from
heaven. Clyde, like the others, chewed his strip until
the flavor was gone.

They talked around the fire a long time, about
what had happened, about what they'd do for water
and food, how seven people could get through the
night with only five sleeping bags. Rocks were still
rumbling out of the North Fork, so there was little
chance of striking out before morning.

Since noon, the clouds had moved back in with a
vengeance. When rain started spluttering in the fire,
Amy got up and covered Ben with a sheet of plastic,
tucking it in all around him.

Clyde's spirits dived right along with the weather.
Every quarter hour or so someone checked the water
level on the stick they'd screwed into the mud, re-
porting that it was up, then down again, then up.
Like a yo-yo, Clyde thought. Steve said it was probably raining over the headwaters.

Clyde got even more nervous when Steve twisted
around to study the silty edges of their shrunken
refuge. His face was a cinch to read.

"How many of us could stuff ourselves into that

118

cavity up in the rocks? You know, where you and Neale got water this morning," Steve asked Audrey.

She glanced up at the cliff rising from the North Fork canyon, her forehead wrinkling. "No more than four. A tight squeeze at that."

"If we have to put you and the kids up there, I want you to go."

Audrey shook her head. "The others, yes. I'm staying with you."

"We'll see . . . all right. Now, what about food? What's left?"

Audrey and Amy had laid things out earlier, with Audrey making jokes about their well-stocked pantry.

"We have enough for two skimpy meals—I think," she said grimly. "Then we either hunt or fish, and this place isn't exactly noted for its game."

Steve grinned as he raised a forefinger. "Snails. There's a species of snails living here in the Narrows that isn't found anywhere else in the world, did you know that?" He showed them how big on a fingernail. "Little bitty guys. Attach themselves at springs, seeps. Ever done snails, Audrey?"

Rick raised his eyebrows. "You kidding? Amy wouldn't eat one even if *she* was endangered."

"That's right," she said, inching closer to the fire. "Oh, brrrrr! I'm never going to be warm again." She hugged her knees to her chest and shook so hard

119

Clyde felt sorry for her. If Rick wasn't interested in keeping her warm, maybe he'd apply for the job.

Audrey reached across him for the coffeepot and poured the end of the chocolate into a cup for Amy. "Don't argue," she said, "just drink it. Afterwards, set the cup by the coals and it'll warm your hands even when it's empty. Survival Tip Number Nine."

A minute later, with everyone quiet and staring at the fire, Audrey said, "Isn't it interesting what people think about in a crisis? During the worst of it, when I was sure we'd just be carried off, I found myself worrying about who'd take care of my parakeet." She looked up at Steve. "Isn't that ridiculous, to be worrying about that parakeet . . . when Frank . . ." She stopped in mid sentence, shrugged. "Oh well."

Clyde wondered who Frank was and why he came second to the bird.

"Did you really think you were going to die?" Rick asked. "I guess I never got that scared."

"Well, *I* did," Amy admitted. "And I don't think it's dumb to worry about a parakeet. I thought about my animals, too." Suddenly she smiled. "Guess what Ben told me. When he was in the tree, you know? He said he kept thinking about the ten bucks I owe him. He figured if he died, I'd just get away with it, never have to pay him back." She picked mud off her jeans as she talked. "Can you believe he'd be thinking about a thing like that?"

"I prayed so hard," Neale said as the sky rumbled all the way across. "And I still don't know—"

She quit without finishing when Steve said, "I know the place they camped. I expect your folks made it through fine."

Clyde didn't want to admit he was thinking about his mom—praying to her, even—and was glad when Steve changed the subject back to *Physa zionis*, the unique canyon snail Jason and he had hoped to see. How would there be any snails after floods sandpapered the Narrows? No way!

Finally Rick said what they were all thinking: "We could be trapped here for days if the weather doesn't change. There isn't a helicopter made that could set down in here."

"Don't mention it." Steve got stiffly to his feet, shook out his legs. "The rain isn't serious yet, Rick. Why don't we get after that log?"

Minutes later, Steve and Rick were hacking away on a big log that had been driven into the ground below the cottonwood. While they used the hatchet, Clyde carried, then stacked and rotated the wood tepee fashion over the coals to let it dry out. Steve was right. They needed to keep busy.

In spite of the weather, Amy and Audrey threw two sleeping bags near Ben and crawled in. Clyde wished in the worst way that he could sack out, but Steve had another job lined up.

"But what about giardiasis?" Clyde asked when

Steve told him to fill pots right out of the river. Everything Jason and he had read warned about drinking the water unless it came out of springs.

"We'll boil hell out of it," Steve said. Then, turning to Neale, "You kids might try up there where you and Audrey got water this morning. It tasted okay to me."

Neale gave Clyde a resigned look as she stood up and reached for the empty coffeepot. Adding a couple of pans from Audrey's storage, they filled everything at the Deep Creek edge, where Neale told Clyde about the neat place she and Audrey had discovered earlier.

"There was just a trickle, but we collected enough for coffee," she told him.

"How'd it taste?"

"Terrible, if you want to know."

Neale's "neat place" was up behind a jutting of rock, hidden from view unless you were looking up from the North Fork canyon. Clyde wasn't sure he could make it with his leg, but Neale promised he could so they took off.

A ragged incline, then some skinny ledges and handholds led them up the face of the cliff. "Where you taking me?" Clyde asked more than once. "My feet don't fit on those little places like yours do."

"Come on, just don't look down."

"This is suicide. You sure I can get up there?"

Neale waited, gave him a hand. "If Audrey made it, so can you."

Clyde sagged with relief when they got to the weathered, hollowed-out place. It was shallow, though high enough to stand in and with a good ledge. The sandstone inside was pitted and rough from erosion.

He shivered, noticing right away that it was colder there above the river, but Neale's expression as she unzipped Rick's jacket and took out a plastic bottle made the climb worthwhile. He could see she considered this *her* place, the way Ben would.

"Oh, don't tell me," she said, running her fingers along the overhang. "It's not even dripping now, is it?"

He looked down, took a step. "There—" He pointed at a wet spot on the rock that was obviously building up minerals.

Neale moaned, said a couple of words his mom didn't allow in the library.

"Let's see—" He struck a pose. "A quick calculation tells me your quart canteen will be filled . . . at four drops a day . . . in about forty years. Allowing for evaporation." Having settled that, he sat down on the ledge and arranged his leg so he'd be halfway comfortable.

"So you got something better to do?" She plopped the bottle down between them.

"Not hardly. Unless I fall asleep . . . which isn't likely with all the activity." He pointed at the bottle.

Neale let herself smile. "Yeah, but watch. If it rains, it'll fill a lot faster than four drops per."

Clyde rubbed his knee, which was swollen to half again its size. How on earth was he going to hike out a half dozen miles tomorrow? He looked at Neale, sitting there biting her nails, and tried for something more positive. "If it rains, we've got ourselves a nice little shelter, anyway."

Déjà vu. He'd said the same thing about the cave. Deciding he should take notice, he checked around, ran his fingers over the surface behind them. There were little pockets of sand everywhere.

"Look at this." He put a pinch of sand in her hand. "How do you suppose it got there? We're at least twenty-five feet up from that river."

She poked the fine grains around in her palm. "Maybe it blew in."

"Maybe it didn't."

He looked down at the gushing North Fork, then across to the other side of the canyon, hardly more than spitting distance from where they sat. Could a flood deposit sand that high up? A thrill in his chest pulled him back from the edge.

When Neale went to work on her chipped fingernail polish again, Clyde leaned back and closed his eyes. He'd never been so hammered in his life. He could sleep if she didn't talk. Even on that cold, hard rock he could sleep like a baby.

"You know what's really bugging me?" she asked.

Oh, no, she wants to talk.

"Nobody's even worried about my folks. Nobody cares. They could be wiped out." He felt a shudder go through her. "You'd think Rick—"

For some seconds her voice lost out to the North Fork, then he roused himself to say, "Not true. I've thought about your folks plenty." Well, some.

"Do you think they were okay there? I wonder how big that cave is. But look what happened to you and Ben. My mom could never climb a tree—she's thirty pounds overweight."

"We were the mavericks, taking chances on two rivers," Clyde answered mechanically, not opening his eyes.

"You know, back there when Audrey was talking about her parakeet and the stuff people think about?"

She's on a roll!

"All I could think about that whole time . . . was my mom."

He opened his eyes to see her drawing her feet up under her. She was staring off. "I haven't been nice to her since I was—oh, about nine."

Clyde shifted his leg, grinning in spite of himself. "How come?"

"I don't know." She stuck a finger in her mouth

and worked on the polish with her teeth. "We fight."

"Maybe you're too much alike."

"I fight with my dad, too, so how do you figure?"

"You like to fight."

Clyde leaned back again. "I don't know anybody who doesn't fight with their folks. I do. Jason does. Mom says a good disagreement clears the air. She claims it's the way kids sharpen their teeth so they can get along in the world."

Neale looked slightly pained. "I'm not talking about that kind of nicey-nice . . . disagreement!" She bounced the edge of her hand on her leg. "I get so mad at my mom I could tear her eyes out."

"Hmmmm. That's pretty mad, all right. So you're probably thrilled you got to be with us instead of them, huh, and have all these adventures."

She turned away with a disgusted noise that annoyed him even more.

He straightened. "I'll tell you something. When I was pasted to that tree holding on to Ben, I was thinking plenty about my mother. And I probably *started* being nice to her when I was nine."

"Okay, *okay!* So . . . what'd you think about her? I mean, were you just seeing her face or what?"

"This sounds conceited—big-time conceited—but I wondered what she was going to do without me. They're divorced. And I live with her."

Suddenly they were giving each other undivided

attention. In fact, she sat there and stared at him a little too long.

"Are you their only kid?" she asked finally.

He nodded.

"Me, too." He watched her chalk up a score: They had something in common.

"So where's your dad?"

"He's around. He's a cop. A *detective* he always wants me to say."

"Do you see him sometimes?"

"No more than I have to."

She pushed back her hair, a curly mess, and let her eyes show for once. In the dead light they were a strange slate blue.

"So—actually—you hate your old man the way I hate my mom?"

Clyde shrugged, wondering why girls like her always have to know everything. Amy had said Neale was in therapy. They teach you to turn everything inside out in therapy.

"Yeah, but see"—she looked past him—"I don't really hate her. I was scared to death I'd die . . . then she'd go on the whole rest of her life thinking I hated her."

Clyde exhaled noisily. Should he tell her to go suck a rock? "So what do you want me to believe. You hate her or you don't?"

She jerked her legs out from under her and slung

127

them over the side, toppling the canteen so she had to make a grab for it. "You believe anything you like!" She might as well have said, "Go to hell!"

"Hey, come on. I'm not trying to—but I feel like you're pulling my leg. The sore one, okay?" He laughed nervously.

"I'm talking serious!" she shouted. "If I run one more time, I'm eligible for Youth Services, that's how serious things are. I just thought I could talk to you, that's all. But I was wrong again, wasn't I? I suppose Amy filled you in. She's good at doing stuff like that."

They sat with their eyes locked until Clyde looked away. "All Amy said was that you had a terrific singing voice. You heard her."

"Humph!"

Clyde lifted the bottle, peered inside, set it back hard. His eyelids were gritty, he was bruised from one end to the other, and he was freezing. Why was he arguing with her?

"It's raining again," Neale said. "God, how depressing!"

Neither of them talked for a minute; then Clyde said, "I was born a klutz, but you already figured that out. If I can say the wrong thing, I'll find a way to say it—every time. It's like . . . it's a talent I have."

"Okay, so I'm sorry, too, but sometimes I just

want to yell. First they tell me I have to get my feelings out, then when I do people can't stand me."

"Yeah, what's a person supposed to do, anyway?"

The rain was picking up fast. He wondered how they'd get down, then decided they shouldn't bother. They'd stay dry here better than anywhere.

All at once he felt Neale's fingers tightening on his arm. "Hey, I'm really scared, no shit."

"Heck, it can't rain forever."

"No, I don't mean that." She was looking right at him now. "I want things to be different—with my folks and me, too. And I swear, after what happened here, I *feel* different. Don't you feel different?"

Clyde nodded her to go on, and she did, rushing the words: "It's like, you know, things at home? It's no big deal anymore! Who cares? My mom makes these contracts with me. *She* makes them! So then we battle it out. Now I've come through these terrible floods and hypothermia, and I'm still alive. I just feel like I've got a second chance, so why go back and get mad over every little thing? It's like, 'Look, Neale, you can handle all that!' You know what I mean?"

Somehow Clyde found the courage to take hold of her hand. He set about rubbing and warming it between his. Before he knew it, she'd thrust another cold trembly hand in beside it and there were two between his big red ones.

He asked, "What's so scary about getting a second chance?"

"I'm afraid, if I get out of this place it'll be the same old thing. I'll forget how I loved them when I was scared, and it'll just be—all over again!" Her voice was imploring. "The only time I'm not scared is when I'm singing . . . and that's the truth."

Clyde felt the scars as soon as his fingers encircled her wrists.

"I did that last year," she said in a voice that hardly made it above the river. "So I'm starting on my third chance, if you want to count."

Up close, even in the bad light, he could see flecks of brown around her irises. He also saw the fear she was talking about, plain as anything. Wide awake now, he ran his thumbs over her wrists again, then over the backs of her hands.

"I'd put money on you," he said, "and I'm a fair judge of horses."

It was as dumb as anything he'd ever said in his life, but he could tell by her face that *she* didn't think so.

Clyde grinned. "Come on, sing me something. I could use a lullaby."

11

Amy sat straight up in the sleeping bag, her heart pounding as if she'd had a nightmare. It's raining! She panicked. Where's Ben?

She craned around. He was still asleep under the plastic sheet, his head buried.

How can it be raining again?

Audrey's bag was empty, but she could hear Steve, Rick—someone—still hacking away at the log. Amy lifted her jacket and pushed her right arm into the sleeve.

Judging by the light, she'd slept awhile, but she felt worse and her mouth tasted like a dirty rag. She pulled the braid out of her collar, rubbed her arms, then fell back against the bag and let rain hit her in the face.

They'd have been coming out of the Narrows by now.

She lay there and listened to Steve's hatchet biting into the wood. Didn't he ever get tired? And Rick, trying to keep up. Poor Rick. Poor Amy. Poor engaged couple! What was happening to them here in the Narrows?

Mentally, she gave herself a shaking, then reached down inside the bag and brought out her shoes. It wasn't a downpour, just millions of silver needles hell-bent for mischief. She never thought she could hate the rain, but right now she did. Give us a break, dammit!

She stepped to the storage bags and dug inside, hoping to find some plastic to throw over the wood, but there were only pint Ziplocs left, one that held black film cannisters labeled "salt," "pepper," "onion flakes."

Amy felt a hunger headache coming on. She looked through the branches to where Audrey was helping Steve and wished she'd come back. Then, unable to find anything, she bunched up both their bags and shoved them into Audrey's pack.

Straightening, she was startled to see someone coming out of the Deep Creek. She stared. Clyde? She knew immediately it wasn't. The guy was carrying a full pack and wearing a baseball cap.

He was keeping to the far side by the cliff, concentrating on every step with a pole a foot taller than he was. Although the rain grayed everything at that distance, she could see he was barely making it.

Amy moved to the edge of the mound where she could get someone's attention, then pointed when Steve finally saw her. By the time Amy looked back, the man had seen them and was changing directions to head across the creek their way.

Amy herself was thrilled to see another human being. For some morbid reason, the idea of someone else's being in the flood made her feel better.

Suddenly Rick dropped the load of wood he was bringing up and veered off toward the Deep Creek, a strange look on his face.

"Gary Rawlings," he yelled, "is that you?"

The guy stopped. Hunched over his pole, he peered at them through the rain. "Chidester?" he hollered back.

Amy stood by with her mouth open. "I can't believe this!" Gary was a fraternity brother of Rick's, one of her favorite people. He leaned there a minute as if catching his breath, then shook water off his cap and came on.

Rick shouted, "Only crazy people hike during flood stage!"

"Look who's talking!" Gary's trademark—a broad, moon-faced smile—brightened the whole blooming confluence.

In his early twenties like Rick, Gary was a real

Eagle Scout kind of guy, and the two had been close friends forever, right up until he left the frat house to get married. Amy knew it tested Gary's good nature, but even to his face Rick called him "a nice Mormon boy."

"Why's he alone?" Amy asked Rick. "Where's Debbi?"

"I don't know, but he sure looks beat."

By the time he reached them, Amy knew he'd been through something. He could hardly walk, his pants were torn. His normally clean-shaven face was stubbly and dirt-smudged—a mosaic of emotions.

Rick took the pole out of his hand and tossed it up on the mound, telling him he looked like a piece of distressed merchandise. They helped him up, got off his pack, pointed him toward what was left of the fire. His boots looked heavy as rocks on his feet, but he covered the few steps before collapsing.

Amy threw a quick look at Rick. Gary was crying. She had her arms around him in a second, saying, "Oh Gary, wasn't it awful?"

Then Rick was down beside him, his own face tight with feelings.

"Sorry—didn't mean to do that," Gary said, smearing tears and dirt across his face. "I was just so glad to see someone. Then . . . find out it's *you*!" He mopped up with his sleeve. "I didn't think anyone could be alive in here . . . wasn't sure *I*'d get

134

out . . . Jessica's only ten months old, you know? That's all I been thinking about, Debbi and my kid."

Steve was by then noisily clearing his throat. "We've all cried," he said. "You wouldn't be much of a man if you weren't affected."

"Thanks." Same old Gary! Then he recognized Ben, who was still asleep. "You've got *him* with you?"

Amy nodded, tight-lipped.

A minute later, Steve came over and put out his hand. "Gary, I'm Steve VanLengren. You'd better stay the night, rest up. Weather's too uncertain to be in that water."

"Oh, excuse me—" Amy got up. "And this is his wife, Audrey VanLen—I'd better let you say it."

"I'm Audrey Heins. How would I manage a name like VanLengren?" Then to Gary, "Did you come in by yourself?"

Gary got to his feet in jerks, with Audrey protesting the whole time that he shouldn't stand.

"No, I was with two other guys, Lewis and Rostkowski. I don't think you know them, Rick—guys from the lab—but I was having so much trouble with tendonitis I didn't want to go on. Sliding off those rocks yesterday killed my ankles. Plan was that I'd, you know, get an early start, meet them at the Grotto." The rain had let up, but a shudder took Gary's shoulders when he said, "I know what they're thinking now."

135

Hugging the fire, a sleeping bag around him, Gary explained that he'd made camp on a high sandbar and had been wakened by the storm. He'd climbed to a pothole in the rocks that he'd spotted earlier. He'd hoisted up his pack with a piece of rope he had along, hooked it over some scrub brush above his head, then spent the next ten hours crouched in that little cradle of rock. "When it hit"—Gary's arms made big circles—"that water rolled over me like I wasn't even there. Even now, I don't know how I pinned myself into that place—an *indentation* is about what it was.

"You should have heard me pray. I even promised to go on a mission if I got a call. Don't laugh, Rick, I did! I was promising everything. And my rear end"—he pounded on his behind—"you could do an autopsy. I mean, I'm dead from here to here."

"Have you had anything to eat?" Amy asked.

"Too scared to be hungry. I still have water, some other stuff. I stopped a while back and finished the cookies Debbi packed for me."

They laughed when Rick said, "What kind of cookies? Describe them."

Gary looked over at Audrey. "How about you guys? You okay on food?"

"Rations are pretty lean," Steve said, "and we're short a couple of sleeping bags. There's a long, cold night coming up, but we've got lots of wood and all the hot water in the world. Once we settle out the solids."

"Listen," Audrey interrupted, "the food you have is yours. We're not going to kill you in your sleep or anything."

"Heck no," he shook his head, "anything I've got we'll divide, you bet!"

"Don't look now, you guys, but it's stopped raining," Rick said. "You brought us luck. Hey, Rawlings, did you bring your harmonica?"

Gary looked injured. "My company isn't enough?"

Rick and Gary traded pokes, then went through some dumb fraternity handshake that looked like cow milking to Amy. When Amy said so, Rick hooked her around the neck and pulled her in for an ardent kiss.

Gary rolled his eyes at Audrey. "You can tell they're not married yet, can't you?"

It was dark by the time they finished talking. Everyone was there now, sitting or standing around the fire, smelling the chicken soup.

"This a Mom-and-Pop operation we got here?" Steve growled, doling out apricots like playing cards. "Nobody else knows how to cook?"

"If you snore that loud tonight," Neale warned Clyde with a toss of her mucky hair, "I'm gonna stuff my shoe in your mouth."

"I got a big mouth," he came back, "but it's not a size nine!"

They'd been sniping at each other ever since they came back with their quarter inch of gritty water. Neale claimed Clyde had fallen asleep and blocked her way so she couldn't get down from the grotto. *His* story was that she had snuggled up so close he couldn't move. Amy had grinned, figuring they were both telling the truth. Clyde was being the kid who dipped the pretty girl's hair in the inkwell. Neale— a world-class squealer—was happy to keep it all going.

Audrey had just begun pouring the soup into cups when Gary looked up and asked if it would be all right for him to offer a prayer. He glanced around— self-consciously, Amy thought—and said, "You guys don't know how glad I was to see you today. It was like, you know, like a miracle or something."

For once Clyde and Neale shut up.

Steve nodded thoughtfully. "You're right, we should." There was silence, then he said, "As youngsters at home, we all held hands around the table when my dad said grace. Do you want to do it that way?" He took Amy's hand on one side, Clyde's on the other.

Audrey left her soup and sat down between Rick and Ben. The sound of rushing water filled the spaces.

"Our Father in Heaven," Gary began in a loud

voice, "we bow our heads before Thee and thank Thee for keeping us safe from harm. Give us strength to carry on, to be patient and tolerant one with another. Bless us with wisdom and clear minds in this crisis so we may return to our families."

Gary paused and Amy opened her eyes, but he wasn't finished yet.

"We ask Thee, Father, to bless this food we are about to partake of, that it will nourish and strengthen our bodies. Please watch over us and all who need Thy help here in the Narrows. These things we ask in the name of Thy son, Jesus Christ. Amen."

Neale said, "Amen," too, and they squeezed each other's hands.

The prayer was comforting, but a flutter in Amy's stomach reminded her that they were at the bottom of the Narrows with all the uncertainties still intact. They were less than halfway.

Ben, rubbing an apricot on his jeans, broke the silence. "I hate apricots with sand!" and the look on his face made everyone laugh.

Dinner was mostly finger food—a small can of salmon and two bagels, courtesy of Gary Rawlings, who insisted that they share it. They also divided one package of chicken noodle soup eight ways by passing three cups around the circle and taking turns.

The water in the containers and the coffeepot had settled out half mud after standing all afternoon.

"And maybe more," Steve said when the time came to fix the soup. They'd filtered the water through a red bandana, then boiled it a good while besides. Even so, Lipton's Instant Chicken Noodle was a new experience mixed with Deep Creek floodwater.

Steve made a big thing of smacking his lips over the first taste. "Hmmm, delicious! Audrey, you've outdone yourself this time. Except you forgot to pluck the chicken."

He handed it on to the next lucky guy, who happened to be Amy. She took a few swallows, made a face. "She also left on the feet."

Making the rounds past Rick and Gary and Clyde, the chicken—part by body part—was reconstructed until Ben was scared to taste it.

"Not me!" he howled. "Not with the beak and all that stuff."

Even with complaints, the soup was gone in five minutes, with Ben getting a good share of it. The little chunks of meat and the noodles tasted wonderful to Amy, although the whole meal was hardly more than an appetizer.

Later, with sleeping bags over their shoulders and everyone sitting so close they touched, Rick said, "Tomorrow morning when we aren't home, our folks will go crazy. Suppose they've heard anything yet?"

"With a flood this magnitude? Sure," Steve answered. "I'll bet there was a news crew at the mouth all day. All afternoon, anyway."

"Going crazy is right." Gary's forehead bunched up. "Poor Debbi. She's such a worrier anyway. Maybe I should have gone on today."

"*Right this minute* my mother thinks I'm dead. She'd have to," Neale added in a tight voice. "If we could get down to the Grotto, I'd go tonight."

"They're okay," Steve said. "I'd be willing to bet on it. Across from the Grotto there's a great big slope with ledges and overhangs. You can get way up from the water over there. It's safer than where *we* are."

Audrey took Neale's hand and patted it between hers. "Your folks are fine and you must quit worrying. They're worrying enough for both of you."

Suddenly Neale blurted out, "Does anybody care if I sing?" She pulled away from Audrey. "If I could just get my mind off—it just helps, you know what I mean? Why don't we all sing something?"

Clyde made a Jack Benny face. "Oh, don't tell me that girl wants to sing again!"

Neale kicked him.

"She put me to sleep up there. What was that great ballad you sang? About Sir Patrick Spens, this dude who ends up at the bottom of the sea, fifty fathoms deep. A really comforting number for the Narrows."

"So I sing ballads! That's my thing. Just shut your ears—I'll do something else."

"Go ahead," Amy said. "I love your voice. But do

141

it right now. In an hour we'll all be asleep."

"That's what I'm telling you," Clyde muttered.

Neale smacked him a second time. Then, hooking her hair behind her ears, she sat up in her Charlie Chaplin clothes and let her hands fall in her lap. It was as if invisible chords came down and lifted her into performing position. When she opened her mouth, Amy's chills arrived in triplicate.

"I gave my love a cherry without a stone,
I gave my love a chicken without a bone. . . ."

Her voice was clear, tremulous, of such quality that Neale the fourteen-year-old was instantly transformed into Neale the singer.

"I gave my love a ring that has no end,
I gave my love a baby with nooooooo cryin' . . ."

"There's that chicken again," said Ben.

"All right." Neale glared at him. "Since you're so smart, you have to sing the second verse with me. It's a riddle, see?"

Clyde said, "Hey, Ben, another riddle!"

Neale went right on lining out the words to the second verse, and then they all sang it together:

"How can there be a cherrrrrry without a stone?
How can there be a chicken without a bone?

How can there be a ring that has no end?
How can there be a baaaaaby with no criiieeeyin'?"

They were heavy on baritones and Ben piped sort
of tunelessly over the others, but nobody cared.

On the final verse, Neale's clear, bell-like soprano
coaxed echoes from the rocks.

"A cherry when it's bloomin', it has no stone,
A chicken when it's pippin', it has no bone,
A ring when it's a rollin', it has no end,
A baby when it's sleepin', there's no cryin'."

The notes went all the way up to heaven—which
tonight was *T*-shaped and sprinkled with stars. In
spite of the weird clothes and wild hair, Neale had
never looked so pretty, Amy thought, as she did
right then. Her audience clapped long and hard.
Even Clyde, who shouted, "More! More!"

A little later when Gary dug out his harmonica,
the music went from English ballads to country blues
to old favorites. They sang and sang. Although the
air grew damp and cold, for whole minutes Amy
could forget they were stranded.

It was three A.M. when Amy stood and looked
over the encampment of bodies. Ben had had a fit
over having to share a bag with Neale, but they

143

were the logical ones. Excluding them, musical bags had been going on all night as the others took turns sitting up and feeding the fire.

The first thing Amy did was step over Steve and Clyde and head for the "bathroom." Girls to the right, boys to the left, had been Audrey's idea, but it was so cold pulling down her pants Amy was tempted to wait. "Better now than later," she told herself. Rick's turn at the fire came next, but she planned to take his shift since he hadn't slept the last thirty-six hours.

As the night wore on, Amy tried to concentrate on "Things to do before October 10." If she just had a pencil and paper! Rick would be proud of her if she ever made a list she didn't lose.

In the end she couldn't concentrate. She was either too hot on one side or freezing on the other or shifting to avoid the smoke. She also found herself covering every grueling mile remaining of the Narrows, trying to imagine how it would be getting out.

Knees drawn up tight, Amy listened to the night sounds of the Narrows and sucked on the side of her hand. In spite of the seven other people, she felt really truly alone. All along she'd been telling herself that marrying Rick would take care of the lonely feelings, but she didn't believe that anymore. It was scary to be undertaking a lifetime hike with a guy you suddenly didn't know very well. Somehow, they'd

144

let each other down on this trip—or they'd let each other *see*. Maybe that was it.

The sky had begun to lighten by the time Gary got up. Gathering boots, socks, sleeping bag in his arms, he carried them all to where Amy was sitting against the cliff.

"Put that around you," he said, tossing her the bag.

"Thanks, great! We'll share." It gave her goose bumps to see him shake. "Did you sleep well here at the Zion Sheraton?"

"My ankles feel a lot better this morning."

"I wondered why you were wearing boots."

"Yeah, bad ankles. You should see me on ice skates."

He pulled on his socks and boots, then scooted close and got one end of the bag around him. Amy was glad for his warmth and company both.

"When's the big day?" he asked pretty soon. "Debbi says she's buying a new dress. I say she isn't. Don't you have something she can borrow?"

Amy grinned. "You cheapskate!" Then she said, "On the calendar our big day is the tenth of next month."

"What kind of answer is that?"

Amy tossed a stick into the fire. "Tell me the truth, Gary. Can you see me married?"

"Sure, why not?" And then, "I can see Rick mar-

145

ried. He's been in love with you since you were sixteen."

"The year I got out of braces."

"Yeah, it was those nice, even teeth."

"How do you like being married?" Amy asked after a silence. "You know what I mean—being a family man, all that."

"Well, most of the time, I like it. It's not easy, I can tell you that. The bills come in. . . . The kid screams half the night. Debbi wants to see a movie and I'm too tired, or there's a paper due and her mother's sitting there talking when I want to study. Sure, there are times when I just want to . . . walk out the door."

"But you don't."

"Nope. They're my whole life."

The fire popped. Amy watched as a little patch of red exploded into flame.

"I don't know if I'm going to feel that way . . . about Rick and me. Being down here, having all this happen, I feel as if—how can I say it?—I feel as if I want to do more with my life. Am I making sense? Gary, life's so short and there are so many things I want to do. What if we get married and I never get to be a vet, for instance? You know how it goes—"

"Yeah, the kids come along—bam, bam, bam!"

"I love kids, don't get me wrong, and taking care

146

of my babies at the zoo just gets my mother hormones screaming sometimes, but . . ."

Gary laced up his boots. "In other words, you're getting cold feet."

Ruefully Amy said, "My feet haven't been warm since I hiked in here."

"Does Rick know what's going on?"

"I don't know. He just kind of plans and goes ahead. Things fall into place because he says they should. I honestly don't think he *thinks* the way I do . . . or broods, whatever it is. And he'd be mad if he heard us talking like this."

"Shall I change the subject?"

"No, it's okay. I love Rick. I just don't know if we're, you know, heading the same direction. That's the only advice my dad ever gives me. 'Just make sure you're heading the same direction,' he says. Now what's that supposed to mean?"

Gary stared into the fire. He was a wonderful listener, but for once Amy wanted him to talk.

"With Debbi and me," he said finally, "it's like, she's my other half. Like our names were right there together in some ol' book up in the sky, and all I had to do was date around until I found her."

He turned to Amy with a grin. "Is that dumb enough? Heck, I don't know how to explain it." He pulled at the tops of his rag wool socks. "But if you don't feel like you're two halves of the same apple, seems to me you're not doing Rick any favors."

Amy studied Gary's profile. So that's how it was with them. Two halves, the same apple. It could never be that simple for her.

Her stomach growled, as if cued by the mention of food.

"Whoaaaa." Gary looked down. "Another country heard from."

Amy laughed, knowing he'd been serious as long as he could.

"When we get out of this place, Amy, let's get ourselves one of those giant fourteen-ounce steaks—medium rare—with Cowboy Sauce. You and Rick and Debbi and me. What d'ya say?"

"Ooooh, don't do that!" She could feel the saliva pooling under her tongue. "Unless you've got mushrooms on mine."

12

Rolling over in the sleeping bag, Clyde was hit by pain that made him suck in his breath. He lay there a minute, panting, hoping it would pass.

How am I going to walk?

When he dared move again, he lifted up to see if anyone else was awake.

Amy was asleep sitting up, her head flopped down on Gary's chest, scarf over her nose. Gary's face was a blank, but he smiled and pointed skyward when he saw Clyde. No threatening clouds; he'd already noticed.

The others were still zonked out in their bags.

Clyde tried to get up, but every move sent jabs through his leg. At last he rolled over to face the bag, pushed up on the good knee, and got to his feet for a stiff-legged walk to the North Fork side of the mound.

Shaking with early morning cold, he slid his jeans down for a look. The wound had been oozing. Into someone else's bag—sick! The sight of his own blood turned his stomach. How was he going to hike six or eight more miles when he could hardly stand to put weight on that right leg?

He zipped up his pants, muttering, "What have I done to myself?"

By 5:52 on Rick's watch, the others were up stuffing bags, being quiet out of regard for Ben and Neale, who were still nested together like spoons.

"They're the only ones who slept warm," Amy said, shivering hard.

Building up the fire as Steve and Audrey packed their gear, the guys held a competition for Cave Man. Clyde qualified first, with his wound from the tusk of a wild animal; Gary had the dirtiest, scraggliest beard; Rick was voted "Neanderthal lips." It was a dumb game, but it got them all laughing.

"Rick also has dinosaur breath," Amy complained.

Audrey, who'd been trying to pull a comb through her hair, listened good-naturedly to all the grungy talk.

"Soap, razor, toothpaste," Clyde ticked them off, "artifacts of a previous existence." He flashed onto the sunny corner of their Santa Monica kitchen where he ate breakfast and read the sports page every day. How much he took for granted!

In about one minute they finished the two packs of instant breakfast mixed with the end of Gary's water supply. They joked, calling it their "instant nonmeal."

"What I crave," Clyde said when he got a chance, "is a plate of JB's vanilla French toast, swimming in butter and syrup."

Everyone groaned.

"With a cup of my mom's coffee," he added. "She makes it from beans." The tan color of the Deep Creek reminded him of coffee at home—coffee with just the right amount of cream and sugar. The red water pouring out of the North Fork looked more like the soup off kidney beans.

Suddenly pain shot through Clyde's thigh, causing him to wince and grab his leg.

Steve looked at him with alarm. "Whoa, is it that bad?"

Right away someone got out the aspirin, then Audrey insisted on examining the gouge behind his knee again. She squeezed the rest of the Neosporin into the wound, put on a clean pad, then tied it in place with the same old dirty gauze. "I don't know what good any of this will do once you're in the river."

Then Audrey folded the aspirin tin into Clyde's hand, saying, "You'll need these during the day, for pain and inflammation both, so don't try to be a hero!"

He nodded and thanked her for all the fun.

"That kid's got to get a doctor . . ." he overheard Audrey telling Steve, "and he can't wait forever. It's already infected."

"Gary, come here," she called a minute later. "I think you and Clyde should start out right now. You're going to be slower than the rest of us, so we'll soon catch up." Looking pointedly at Clyde, she said, "You need to get out as fast as you can. This dirty water! The idea of gangrene in that leg just terrifies me, and it's a real possibility without antibiotics."

Gary stood there scratching his head, popping his cap off and on like he was trying to think but not getting far.

Audrey said, "I'm not a nurse, but I once worked in a doctor's office."

"—which is as close as we'll get to a medical opinion down here," Steve added like an endorsement.

Clyde listened. The word *gangrene* suggested amputation, and losing a leg wasn't exactly his choice of fates.

The plan, finally, was for them to go ahead, to wait at the Grotto if Clyde needed help or couldn't hike any farther. Gary's friends would be there— big, strong guys, both of them. And the Dwyers would have extra food, since they were carrying Neale's share.

152

After Gary strapped on his pack, Rick and he exchanged pats on the rear. "If my ankles act up, you may end up carrying me out, so don't be too far behind."

"We'll be right on your tail," Steve assured him.

Clyde looked at Amy, wanting like crazy to hug her good-bye. He pointed to Ben, who was still asleep with his mouth open. "Tell him to be brave . . . like his Uncle Clyde," he said. "And tell him I want a good riddle when I see him next, not one of those dumb ones."

She gave him an A-okay, but the worried look never left her face.

It was just plain depressing wading into the dark Narrows once they left The Forks. Clyde could hear his heart in his ears. If it rained now, there was no place to go. Not here, anyway. He wondered if it was smart to be without Steve, the only one who knew the canyon. They'd decided so fast. *Audrey* had decided. What difference would another hour have made?

Once they adjusted to each other's pace, Clyde found himself checking the walls for ledges and escape routes, but found only freaky flood remains instead. Above their heads, he saw a tangle of driftwood caught in an impossibly high place. Below, there wasn't a speck of moss where floodwaters had rolled through. How would it be to have that wall of water at your back with no place to go? Looking at Gary, feeling the trembling that came through his grip, Clyde figured they both knew too much to enjoy what was left of the Narrows. They just wanted to get out.

On the map the Grotto was shown as an hour's trek from the confluence, but the gummy bottom slowed them down even as it sapped their strength. The only good part was that Clyde's leg felt better in the cold water. Or maybe the aspirin was doing its work.

There was no shouting back and forth, no talk at all as they fought dizziness and the current, struggling to keep their balance. Digging in his pole, hefting one foot after another out of the muck, Clyde thought of moonwalkers. "One small step for man . . ."

How many steps to the Temple of Sinawava? Don't think about it. Too many.

They came to a broad place next where they were bathed with the most amazing pink glow from light filtering in. They looked at each other, then Clyde let his eyes go all the way to the top. The Narrows was a two-faced Janus—beyond beauty one time, monstrous the next.

The first real test was a logjam they could hear before they ever got to it. The water was deeper there where it came crashing in, backed up, finally sluiced through spaces to go roiling out the other side. It made a noise like the falls.

"Scary as hell!" Gary shouted.

At that exact point Clyde's body morphine kicked in. He was no longer aware of his leg. Hanging on to each other for dear life, hugging the cliff, they somehow crawled over a giant boulder, then rock scrambled in and out of the water and over logs whose ends had been pulped like chewed matchsticks.

About midpoint, they could see that the worst of it was still ahead—a twenty-foot stretch of foaming rapids. It's suicide! Clyde thought.

Hooking their legs around the last log, Clyde strapped their sticks across the top of Gary's pack and cinched them tight. They couldn't talk with all the noise, but they grabbed hands for luck before separating, before Gary gamely slid in to take the lead.

The water was up to his chest, the surface alternately sliding into hollows and breaking across his face. Slowly he made his way along the cliff, his left hand searching ahead of him for holds. It took him ten minutes to go ten feet. His expression was grim when he finally signaled Clyde to come on.

Following Gary's example, Clyde slid off the log and pressed into the rock, every muscle tense. The waves lifted him one minute, dashed him down the next in a rhythm that made him lose footing and swallow mouthfuls, but he knew he couldn't let go.

Take it easy, he coached himself, take it slow . . . don't choke, you'll drown!

It might have been fun, another place, riding the waves with only fingertips for suction, but here danger and death overlapped. Clyde was as scared as he'd ever been.

Suddenly, right in front of his eyes, Gary swirled away from the rock and into the river.

Clyde screamed. A wave rolled over his own head. Back for air, he pulled himself up as high as he could to look for Gary. There! His backpack, unclipped, was floating high. He was still in it!

"Swim!" Clyde yelled as river, cliffs, canyon blurred into one watery mass in front of him.

When he next spotted Gary, he was paddling for all he was worth. The pack—his big old awkward pack!—was keeping him afloat.

Clyde's fingers scoured the rock, then closed on an edge from which he pulled himself forward. "Again!" he ordered his hand, blindly searching for another hold. "Keep on . . . keep going! There's no other way out!"

A millennium later, he was into a slight back eddy, where the river, by some miracle, broadened out into calmer water. There he hauled his spastic body out onto a bank where the rocks had been tumbled smooth as loaves by the flood.

Ahead, not thirty yards away, Gary was stretched out like a man shipwrecked. He was facedown and he didn't move. He was still wearing the loaded backpack, from which the walking sticks extended like dragonfly wings.

Clyde's heart leaped. "Gary! You okay?"

Gary raised a hand, let it flop.

"Don't scare me like that!" Clyde hollered, grabbing lungsful of air. "Don't ever do that again."

The polished fat rocks made it hard to walk, but he was soon dropping down next to Gary. "Are you all right?' he asked again as he patted Gary's head, the need to touch being stronger than anything else now that they were safe.

Gary sat up as if with enormous effort, and began loosening his straps.

Clyde helped him out of his pack, saying, "How are the rest of them gonna make it? Ben . . . jeez, he's so little."

"Steve will be smart enough to use a rope," Gary said. "We weren't." He pulled up his shirt, rung it out and wiped his face. When he finally looked at Clyde, he started laughing. "Was that an epic or not?"

Beyond the logjam it wasn't uncommon to plunge into holes that dropped them to their chests or shoulders. The cold took their breath every time, and they fought being lifted right off their feet. Mirac-

157

ulously, there was often a gentler current where it was deepest, but they still wrenched each other's wrists trying not to let go.

"Still with me?" Gary would call out in the middle of things, his backpack swaying dangerously or floating up behind when he'd release the clip.

"Can't leave my pack," he shouted in Clyde's face at one point. "Cost too much."

"I'd take turns—" Clyde yelled back, never finishing because Gary said, "Don't worry, I'm makin' it!"

If they could just get to the Grotto, where there were people! Clyde pictured a fire, water, food. He prayed for each decent bank that came along and allowed them to get out of the river.

When they recognized the Kolob Creek coming in on their right, they decided to rest again. As at The Forks, flood evidence was everywhere—driftwood in haphazard piles, bare-rooted trees, gullies and heaped-up gravel.

"Land!" Gary shouted with a rueful laugh as they stumbled onto a sandbar.

They dropped down again, intending to rest, but were so cold out of the river they were miserable. Here where the canyon opened up, they at least had a chance to study the sky. Clyde's heart sank. Same old cloudy pattern. If he had to put money on the weather, he'd have said "rain."

"Not that we don't have enough to worry about," Gary muttered.

For the next fifteen minutes they hardly exchanged a word.

The Grotto, when they got there, was empty. They knew before they even crossed the sandy apron leading up to it. Inside, hearing it echo like a big old empty classroom, Clyde was ready to fall down and cry.

There were clear signs that the Grotto itself had been flooded. Underfoot, the mix of sand and silt was spongy everywhere they stepped. Clyde's chest tightened as he thought of Neale.

"Nobody cares," she'd told him yesterday, when all he'd wanted to do was sleep.

Gloom settled in. "What do you think?" Clyde asked.

"If they had time to get across to the other side, they were okay. Or if they camped over there."

Clyde looked at the gentle slope opposite with its ledges and banks.

"Hey," Gary said, taking off toward the rear of the Grotto. "There's something back in there." Clyde trailed along, his leg throbbing.

Someone had left a pile of neatly folded clothes. And food! Gary bent down and picked up a can of pears, a bag of wheat rolls, a Ziploc bag containing

159

matches. Between a sweater and windbreaker they found a note scratched in charcoal on a paper bag.

"My gosh, look at this," Gary said as he pulled it out.

"They made it then! Man, what a scare!"

They moved toward the entrance, where the light was better.

" '10 OK,' " Gary read, " 'praying . . . Out Mon. 6:00 A.M.' "

He looked up. "That's today, and they're only an hour or so ahead of us. Ten—that's a bunch."

"Yeah, and it looks like they all signed their initials."

" 'R. L.'—that's Bob Lewis, the guy I work with," Gary said. "How come they didn't wait for me? Here's 'H. D. and L. D.' "

"Neale's folks! Got to be. Their name's Dwyer."

Gary tipped the paper to the light. "Who's 'J & H. T.'—and here's 'J & W. A.'?"

Clyde shrugged. "I don't know. Other people, I guess."

"Two more. 'L. and B. L.' and—" Gary's broad pancake face split with a smile. "Rostkowski! Look, he signed his D. R. real big like John Hancock! That figures—what an egomaniac!"

Still shivering themselves, they went back and inspected the clothes. Small sizes, everything.

"Neale's," Clyde concluded. "Can you imagine how

they felt when they piled this stuff here? Not knowing?" Clyde tidied up the stack. "I can't believe they went off and left her, can you?"

"They all cleared out. Must have had a reason. Here I was expecting breakfast."

Not to be disappointed, they helped themselves to a roll apiece, then left the rest for the others.

While Clyde sat down near the entrance to chew up a couple more aspirin, Gary climbed around to the right of the Grotto and disappeared into the brush.

"Look what I found," he said, coming back a minute later with a cracked and sandy boiled egg on the palm of his hand.

Clyde made a face. "You going to eat it?"

Gary sat down by Clyde. They looked at it, both gave it a sniff. "It smells okay to me," Gary said with a shrug.

He peeled the egg with great care, then divided it with his thumbnail. The two of them ate it—sand and all.

13

Amy was so thirsty her throat ached. "My kingdom for a Coke," she'd been saying, "or anything wet!"

Rain wasn't exactly what she had in mind, but they hadn't reached Big Springs, the next map stop after Goose Creek, when the sky opened up and water came down in sheets, dappling the slick surface of the river with a million pinpoints.

"Look for high ground!" shouted Steve, getting a grip on Ben, who was presently piggyback.

If Gary hadn't seen them and hollered, they'd have missed each other in the downpour. When Amy finally spotted them, the two were crouched under a brush shelter high in a gully across the river. "Cross over, cross over!" they kept yelling and motioning.

Ben whooped and waved back, in spite of rain smacking him in the face.

Crossing at a bend where the water actually appeared to tilt, Amy was taken a dozen feet farther downstream than she intended. The only one who made a straight crossing was Steve, who claimed Ben made good ballast.

With rain sliding down her face and neck, Amy waited for Ben to force his swollen feet back into sneakers, then helped him climb the forty or so feet into the wooded gully. Gary and Clyde were dragging in brush to extend the lean-to when they got there.

"Had enough rain?" Gary asked, grinning big to see Rick.

Right away Clyde put an arm out for Ben, and the two wrestled and hugged.

"Oh, wow, gnarly!" gushed Neale, ducking inside. "This is cool."

The others squeezed in, Steve on his hands and knees, Rick untying the bags from the daypack first and tossing them in. Clyde and Gary pushed in on the ends where it was drippy.

"I figured you boys would be out of the Narrows by now," Steve said, scooting close to Audrey. "How's the leg doing?"

"The same. Swelling might be worse." Clyde put his hands around his knee. "Thing is, we got so lonesome for old Ben we just had to wait."

Ben crawled over Neale and pushed in next to

Clyde. "Me, too," he said, his eyes shining.

"We could see it coming"—Gary shouted from his end—"and with that narrow stretch just ahead . . . man, I wouldn't be in there now for nothin'!"

"How'd you get through that logjam?" Clyde wanted to know.

"I almost didn't!" Neale screeched. "I dropped in clear over my head—huh, you guys? And swallowed all that icky water." She shuddered. "Noise and spray . . . you couldn't see, you couldn't hear." She looked down the line at Steve. "If you'd let go of me, I'da been dead, that's all."

Gary handed around two plastic bottles filled with fresh water and they took turns drinking as they talked. Audrey was thrilled to hear there was a spring nearby—for her tea and to clean up.

The rain continued to pour and Steve continued to fuss about how they were sitting right in the mouth of a gully. But the shelter was old, so they decided to chance it. Besides, no one had the heart to move.

Being a good sport, being *optimistic* was the name of the game now. Their talk ran to "It's gotta quit sometime," and "Just watch, it'll blow over!" Neale especially, since discovering her folks were alive, had been obnoxiously cheerful. After one long depressing period when they all sat staring at the rain,

164

Neale broke into Annie's song, "Tomorrow," and got them all talking again—mostly about what they'd be doing this time tomorrow.

"Washing the mud out of my hair!" Amy predicted.

Pretty soon Rick got his stove out of the daypack and pumped it up so Audrey could make tea. Steve got a fire going with chips and shavings.

Although thunder rolled up the canyon from below, nobody mentioned the other group of hikers—where they'd be, *if* they'd be out of the dangerous section where high ground didn't exist. Only when she saw Clyde studying the map did Neale ask how long it took to get through the place "where the cliffs go straight up."

"Two hours and some," Clyde said. "And that's average." He'd folded up the map and put it in his pocket without showing her. "You could do it faster if you had to, I bet."

Amy noticed how he'd translated the "2 hrs. 45 min." on the map to "two hours and some"—as considerate a lie as she'd ever heard. For all any of them knew, Neale's folks and the others might be waiting out the rain a quarter hour away at Big Springs. What an irony—if they were that close to each other and didn't know!

Although it never rained as hard again as it did the first hour, it drizzled on and on, with mists crawling up and down the canyon like ghosts. The good part was the warm air, which left them fairly comfortable once their jeans dried. The bad part was being hungry and the misery that went with it.

Everyone tried to keep busy. Amy listened for a while to the Paiute Indian legends Clyde was telling Ben, then combed and braided Neale's hair for her. She watched Rick make precision work of notching and planting a stick, although it was easy to tell what was happening to the river without it. "I go crazy sitting around," he said when someone asked why he bothered.

Clyde, after finishing the aspirin and starting on the Tylenol, was up limping around, collecting firewood. Steve and Audrey talked until she fell asleep on top of a bag. Somehow the hours passed without food or much else that was comforting.

It was going on three when Steve called a meeting. Audrey had just brewed another pot of tea and they'd voted to eat the wheat rolls but save the pears. Amy was glad. Her head was splitting again. She'd have eaten bark if they'd had ketchup.

Steve pulled up a slab of sandstone so he could sit and face the others. He took a roll, handed the plastic bag to Rick.

"We could probably get out today," he said, "but we'd have to leave right away. I'm not hearing rocks in the river anymore, and it's clearing up good, but there's always a risk . . . maybe more than a little. What do you think?"

"You know the river's up, don't you?" Rick asked.

"A couple inches, but from the way that storm moved I'd guess it was worse down in the park than up north over the plateau or Cedar Mountain."

Gary nodded, his mouth full of roll. "I think you're right."

"How do you know that?" Rick asked, looking from one to the other.

"Take a look at the way this area drains." Steve scraped aside leaves to get to the dirt, then drew a map with his finger, showing the North Fork and Deep Creek joining to form the Y at The Forks. He identified the Visitors' Center below, where hikers come out, and Cedar Mountain above and to the left.

"A lot of flash floods in the Narrows originate here." He tapped Cedar Mountain. "Generally the storms move east across the plateau, which explains that second crest coming two hours later on the North Fork."

Steve pulled up his knees. "I think the storm today was more localized, judging from the thunder. Sounded like it was worse south of us." He nodded downcanyon. "If that's the case, the run-off will be light and will drain out pretty fast."

167

Amy wondered if her face showed as much strain as his. Senior member of the group, he knew so much more. . . . Why was he asking them? Why didn't he just say, "This is what we'll do"?

Steve took a breath, went on in a tired voice. "When to leave here, of course, involves all of us unless we split up. A wrong move could have consequences."

"Don't tell me we're stuck here all night?" Neale wailed.

"Yeah, but what's one more night if we get out alive?" Rick confronted her. "I'd rather be safe than sorry, wouldn't you?"

"We have to think about Clyde's leg," Audrey reminded them. "He needs to see a doctor. That's a biggie. We're talking the possibility of . . . well, you know, even gangrene."

"If Clyde and I were in here alone," Steve said, "I'd go for it in spite of the rain. In fact, maybe that's what we should do anyway. How do the rest of you feel?"

All eyes were suddenly on Clyde.

"Don't make *me* decide! I'd rather be alive with one leg—if it came to that—than drown."

"What's he mean?" Ben whispered to Amy.

"If we were well supplied, I'd say we should wait. Unless—"

Amy knew it would be a big "unless."

"—unless it rains all night, all day tomorrow. We're out of food once we finish the pears. What else have we got, Audrey—anything?"

She shook her head no. Then added, "Two tea bags."

"It'll take strength to hike out of here, with that tough section still ahead. Sitting around without any food, we'll get weak in a hurry."

Steve wanted to try it, Amy could tell. The rest, including her, were scared—that's what it amounted to. The flood was too fresh, too horrible in their minds.

"You guys can take off if you want to," Rick said as he got up to feed the fire. "I'm staying!"

"We could make it," Gary said, speaking to Rick. "Debbi'll be crazy not knowing."

"Look, man, she wants you alive, not dead!"

"I like it here," Ben piped up. "This is the best place we've had yet."

"Another possibility is for two of you to strike out without the rest," Steve said. "Gary . . . or anyone . . ."

When they brought it to a vote, only Audrey and Gary raised their hands with Steve.

"All right," Steve said. "That's the will of the majority. Gloomy as the prospect sounds, we're going to spend a third night in the Narrows."

"If I can get some hot water to wash with, I can

survive, but not otherwise!" Audrey's eyes shot sparks as she said it.

Steve laughed and patted her leg. "I'll heat your bathwater myself."

"Neale," Ben said in a weary voice, "guess I have to sleep with you again."

Amy and the others smiled.

"I thought you hated me," Neale teased. "You sure did last night."

"I still do, but I'm sleeping with you anyway."

She made a face. "You better not touch me with those oozy, icky feet."

"I'm not gonna touch you at all!"

Amy thumped Ben on the head.

"Don't forget, we're short another bag after losing Neale's," Steve reminded them as he got up. He handed Audrey his empty cup, rolled up the sleeves of his fatigue jacket and picked up the hatchet. "Think I'll build us a woodpile," he said.

By four o'clock the sky was sunny and blue. At exactly 4:33 P.M. a two-foot crest of water roared by like a loaded freight train, carrying rocks and debris and frothy with mud. They watched it from above, Amy with prickles on her scalp. They'd have been buried had it caught them in the narrow section ahead.

Rick's expression said, "What did I tell you?"

170

Audrey, plainly shaken, buried her face against Steve's shoulder.

"You can't outwit the Narrows," he said. "I guess a person oughtn't to try."

Later, with the light fading, Rick got back into his poncho and announced that he was going to walk up the gulley and stretch his legs.

"Need company?" Amy asked. She grabbed his ankle as he stood.

"Nah, I'm okay, just tired of sitting here listening to Gary's lies."

Gary had a thing or two to say back, then took off with Ben, who was now hobbling around in stocking feet, to give him some rock-throwing pointers. Ben was enormously impressed to know that Gary played baseball in a church league.

Across the fire, Steve and Audrey stood by themselves and talked in low voices. Amy felt sorry for them. Some holiday they were having! You hike the Narrows for peace and solitude, not to acquire a family. How would it feel being outvoted by the crew who'd just eaten up your food and used all your supplies? Worse, how would it feel to be so dead wrong about the river?

A little later, hearing loose rock roll down the slope, Amy left the fire to go meet Rick, wondering—uneasily—if he had any idea at all about what

171

was going on inside her head. Sooner or later they'd have to talk, but not here. Nothing was normal here. She wasn't even sure *how* to talk about what was bothering her, but there was a cold fist tightening on her heart, a terror quite apart from her Narrows experience.

"Where are you?" Amy called out, zipping her jacket as she climbed up the gully.

"Stay there, I'll find you."

Amy was blind from staring at the fire, but she went on toward his voice anyway.

Rick met her with his arms out. She walked right in, holding him close the way she always did. She could feel his heartbeats, hear him breathe, could smell the mix of white gas and perspiration on his skin. Why was he so easy to love?

He lifted her chin and they kissed a long time.

When they moved apart, Amy found herself sniffing at his breath. "What smells so good? Did you find something to eat?" She thought of Gary's luck finding the boiled egg.

Rick didn't answer. He just took her hand and headed her on down.

"Tell me!" she insisted.

"What are you talking about?"

She giggled. "You smell like peanuts . . . or a candy bar or something. Come on, tell me what you had."

Even in the dusk she could see his jaw working.

He gave a funny laugh when he said, "Oh yeah, there was a chunk of something in my pocket."

She slid her hand into his rear pocket and came out with an empty granola bar wrapping. She crinkled it in her fist.

Rick shrugged her off as they picked their way down. "Ben . . . he had a granola bar that first day when you took off mad. You know, when I scared you about the snake." With exaggerated sarcasm he added, "When I acted *childish*."

They were nearly back to the fire when Amy suddenly went livid. Ben had told her he'd had a Hershey's that afternoon.

"What else do you have hidden on you?" She frisked him, plunged her hand in a side pocket and pulled out an unopened granola bar before he could stop her. She'd even paid for those herself!

Grabbing her arm, he steered her away from the shelter. "Shut up!" he hissed. "*You* eat that one. There wasn't enough—"

"Get your hands off me!"

Everyone at the fire stopped talking, but Amy didn't care. "There was a whole box of granola bars! Neale had two, I didn't have any. So how many did you eat the other morning?"

"Amy, this is bull crap. What are you trying to do?"

"I mean it!' she shrieked. "How many?"

Gary came up sweet as a Mormon bishop until he saw how mad she was. "Hey, what's the matter?"

Ignoring him, Amy spun around and accosted Audrey. "How many did you have?"

"One," Audrey answered. "What is this?"

"Steve, how many? I just want to know, I'm counting."

"One, I guess."

"Why are you mad?" Ben asked in a worried voice.

Amy had him by the shoulders next. "What'd you have for a snack with Rick that first day? When Clyde and I went ahead—"

"A Hershey bar."

Gary scuffled to put his arms around her. "Come on, Amy, what's the difference? We're all on edge."

"That's right," Steve said. "Let's not do this."

"No!" Amy jerked free. "I'm *doing* it! Two bars for Neale, one for Steve, one, Audrey." She shook four fingers in Rick's face. "You ate two and were *saving* two. Even a . . . a pack rat . . . thinks about its family!"

Red-faced, furious, Rick took off for the river.

She screamed after him. "We're going to eat this for breakfast and not give you a bite!" She pounded the bar into her palm, then whirled back around. "He went off up there to eat his *dinner* just now. Naturally you want to be alone to eat stolen food!"

174

"Knock it off!" Gary ordered. "You don't have to crucify him."

Half crying, Amy turned on her heel and took off up the gully, where she sank down in the brush. She wanted to die, she was so ashamed of Rick.

She rocked back and forth, arms across her chest, until the hot tears came. She also wanted to die for what she'd just done to him.

The sky was still full of stars when Amy was aware that Rick was unzipping his bag and putting on shoes. Although the smoke rose in a column between them, she could see him shake as he tried to get into his Patagonia jacket. He came stiff-legged to the fire.

"Are you trying to be a martyr?" he said crossly. "You've been up since two—why didn't you wake me? Go on, get in the bag while it's warm."

"What time is it?"

He tipped his wrist to the fire. "Four twenty. You can still get a couple hours, so go on."

Amy stood, squeezed the muscles of her neck. "I ache everywhere."

It seemed unnatural for them to stand next to each other and not touch, but that's what they did. Now that she was standing, Amy could hear the low rushing sound of water again and it depressed the heck out of her.

175

"Amy"—Rick cleared his throat—"why don't you give me any credit?"

She held her breath. *At four in the morning?*

"Because you think I don't deserve any, right?"

"I told you I was sorry."

"But your eyes weren't sorry. I'd sooner be eyeballing a rattlesnake."

Just then Clyde returned from the gully, his light bouncing through the brush. He was making whistling sounds, the kind you make between clenched teeth. He spoke to Rick, got some Tylenol, found a cup. "I'll be back for the changing of the guard," he said as he limped off toward the spring.

Rick took Amy's shoulders. "The half I ate was what I'd saved for you when Neale got hypothermia, remember? You were crying about Ben and said you couldn't eat. I saved that half because I knew you'd need it later on."

"So what are you saying? You saved it for me, but you ate it up there in the gully—"

His arms dropped. "Do you want to listen or not?"

Amy shut up.

"I was up there sitting on a rock and I kept feeling this thing poking me in the ribs. I didn't even remember what it was until I pulled it out. So help me, I didn't think what I was doing, I just ate it. I didn't think about bringing it back and giving everyone a pinch, dammit! I just ate it, is that so bad? I was going to bring out that last granola bar when someone really had to have food. Like with Neale. I saved it for a reserve—in case we were desperate."

Amy looked from Rick's eyes to his lips, then back again. Her impulse was to cover his mouth, to say, "Don't make it worse."

He swung away, walked off. "Go to sleep," he said in a tight voice. "I can't talk to you, I don't even want to."

Amy had her arms around his neck in a flash, hating herself for being so unforgiving. "It doesn't matter anymore, don't you see? It was a very human thing to do, and I should never have attacked you that way. I haven't slept a wink worrying about it!"

He pulled away, his profile stony, then proceeded to pile on enough wood to last the night. "Why are you saving wood now?" His shivers came without interruption. "We'll be out of here . . . or is burning all this dead stuff against your principles like everything else?"

An hour later, with Clyde in the bag Rick vacated, with Rick's head in her lap and him asleep, Amy watched the stars disappear. She thought of Homer's rosy-fingered dawn that she'd read about in tenth-grade English. A soft rosy light was just breaking above the canyon rims.

This morning she could see herself and Rick and

their life together with goose-bump clarity. She wasn't afraid anymore. It had taken an all-night vigil in the inhospitable Zion Narrows, but for the first time in their two-year relationship, Amy knew her own mind.

"Come on, sun!" she kept whispering, urging the hour along. She wanted to get this first day of the rest of her life over with.

14

The Tuesday-morning sun was like a gift. A promise. It gave Clyde hope. He and Ben, whose blisters were also infected, needed sunny skies more than anyone, he decided.

They waded into the Virgin River a little after eight, traveling light, having left all gear behind except ropes, Steve's daypack containing first aid and water bottles, and Amy's sleeping bag in case of emergency.

"It kills me to leave that new pack," Gary had said after an hour's indecision. Finally he'd hidden it high up in the brush, hoping he could talk some ranger into bringing it out on a routine patrol.

"Hey, Ben," Neale shouted after their second crossing, one of the easier ones. "How come you're doing this instead of going to school?"

"Don't ask me!" he answered. "That airplane we keep seeing? I think that's Butler's truant officer. Next time it comes I'm hidin'."

"What about me?" Clyde hobbled out of the river behind everyone else, his purple knee bulging out where he'd had to slit his jeans. "Jason and I were supposed to fly out last night, and I don't have money for another ticket. No cash, the way I look . . . I'll get arrested!"

"You are a mess," Neale said—*she*, who had the only fresh clothes in the group.

Amy hung back to say, "They can smell us coming, that's the worst part."

"Even my skin stinks."

"Is it the mud or what?"

Suddenly they were all noticing the smell and soon realized the canyon, like themselves, was giving off a bad odor.

"Something dead," Gary hollered over his shoulder. "Really putrid!"

Ahead where the smell was strongest, they found the river dammed with boulders the size of foreign cars, with logs and sticks piled everywhere. Luckily, there was room on the right bank to scramble above the logjam.

Below, trapped in the muck and debris, Clyde spotted the bloated body of a dead cow.

"Don't look, you guys!" he cried. Everyone did,

of course, then had to stand there and stare a minute. The carcass loomed rigid where it was caught, the feet on the upper side elevated, stiff, unnatural. It made Clyde sick to look at it.

"Poor thing! How would a cow get in the Narrows?"

"Probably washed in from the plateau," said Steve.

Amy started hiking again. "A lot of little animals died, I bet."

"Not so nice on an empty stomach," Audrey remarked.

With Gary and Rick helping on either side, Clyde and the rest rock climbed even higher to avoid getting back in the water where the smell was so bad. It was a seventy-five-foot detour—painful, too— but neither he nor Ben complained.

They were on the way down a talus slope on the other side when Ben suddenly yelled that the plane was coming back.

"Signal him! Hurry! Get something—quick!"

Amy and Audrey took off running, sliding on the loose rock to get where they could be seen. Audrey unzipped her red jacket and waved it around her head like she was calf roping. Clyde couldn't keep up, but he shouted with the others, for what good it would do.

"Herrrrre! Down here!" He waved his arms over his head. The plane was out of sight in three seconds.

"Did they see us that time?" cried Ben.

Clyde stared after it, breathing hard. "Yeah, maybe. They ought to dip their wings so we'd know."

Rick threw him a sharp look. "What good would that do? They can't launch a rescue during flood stage. The Narrows is a crapshoot right now."

"They'd know someone's still alive in here," Amy disagreed. "That's something. You know how scared our folks are right now?"

Ben heaved a rock. "That pilot could slow down if he wanted to, I bet."

"Like trying to see ants down a well," Gary mumbled.

Steve led off this time, saying, "Come on, troops, we've got five hours of hiking ahead and two wounded. We have to rescue ourselves."

A short while later they were at Big Springs, oasis of the Narrows, where they all got drinks. The place was downright inviting, with bright-green ferns and monkey flowers above their heads and clear, fresh water gushing out of the rocks. Clyde told Amy he was going to spend September right there.

"You guys go on without me. I'll live on the snails. I know they're up there somewhere . . . above the flood line."

"Where? You see any?" Ben wanted to know.

Neale spent her time at the Springs looking for messages from her folks or Gary's friends, but there

182

was no sign anyone had ever been there.

"This makes me too nervous," she told Clyde when they started out again. "I haven't seen a single footprint since we left that gully."

Minutes later they were entering the dark, three-hour long "death strip." The canyon was radically narrow, just as described. The cliffs rose straight up, the rock a mixture of knobby and smooth. There were no features, no weather holes or ledges, that could offer safety.

A terrible oppression came over Clyde, making the hairs on his arms stand of their own accord. "No safe highground" were the words used on the map.

"You okay?" Amy asked Clyde. They'd switched buddies at Big Springs and she was taking a turn with him. Until she flinched, he didn't realize what a tight grip he'd had on her hand.

"Sorry," he said. "Didn't mean to break your bones. Yeah, I'm okay." He could win a liar's contest with that one.

"I'll bet your leg's killing you."

"Some, but I'm already a Tylenol junkie."

"I'm just sick about what happened to your leg," she said, her eyes big and earnest.

He went back to staring straight ahead, wishing again he could take her home with him. She was too nice for Rick. How had they ever got together? No matter, she was with him now, and with his injury and her size they were a good match. Plant the pole, drag a leg, plant the pole . . . keep contact with the ground or off you go. At least it was firm underfoot for a while.

"I never thanked you for saving Ben's life," Amy said out of the blue, "but I decided I could write that kind of stuff easier. Will you give me your address when we get out—and not forget?"

He nodded, then said, "But we'll be moving. And pretty soon, I hope." *What am I saying? Did I hear myself right?*

Now she twisted *his* hand stumbling over a rock. "You are? Where to?"

He held back until she got her balance again, wondering when he'd made the commitment. *During the flood? Just now? But she was waiting . . .*

"We're going up north. To Eureka, where my aunt lives." The words came pouring out, unplanned. It was like listening to someone else talk.

"Is it a transfer or something?"

"No. Wait. Okay . . . back up," Clyde said in a voice that had turned trembly. "Did Gary tell you about promising to go on a Mormon mission? You know, if he came out alive? Did he tell you that?"

Amy grinned. "Kind of joking, though. I don't know if he'd do it."

"I guess we were all bargaining. In my case—" *Why am I telling her this?* he wondered. *Am I just* jerking her around, asking for sympathy? "I wasn't promising God or anything." His throat tightened with each word. "More myself I guess. Mom . . . she needs to get out of Santa Monica. They're divorced, but my dad still comes around. He gets abusive and she ends up crying and depressed for days. And it's just gonna go on, you know?"

The dizzying water slid by like syrup, but Amy's eyes were glued to his face.

"Mom's sister wants her up there to manage a bookstore she owns, but Mom thought I should graduate first."

They had to probe through a boulder field and Clyde measured the pain in perspiration. His underarms were soaked. When they were underway again, Amy surprised him by saying, "Do you think you'll really do it?"

She knew him too well. Saying something was one thing, doing it another.

Fresh pain made him suck in his stomach—a timely reminder. When he'd thought he was going to die, it was "Save me, Mom, save me!" Now— well—he wasn't a kid anymore. She didn't need to plan her life around him the way she'd been doing. Maybe it took a death threat to make him see it, but it was his turn to be unselfish. His mom meant more to him than his best friend. They'd all have to make new friends. That's just the way things were.

Clyde glanced up at the red streaking on the cliffs and seconded his own motion. "We have to move. She's really miserable. I can do my senior year just as well in Eureka . . . and Humboldt College is right next door. We wouldn't have big bucks, but heck, we never did. *Books*, but not bucks."

He could always get another job at minimum wage. Maybe, with a new life, his mother would go out once in a while, meet someone like Steve.

Amy's eyes glistened when she said, "Clyde, you're something. I mean it. There's a girl out there who's going to be so lucky someday."

He felt himself trying to blush. "Aw shucks, ma'am." He did his dumb bumpkin chuckle, but in total seriousness added, "Rick's the one who's lucky."

Amy's eyes filled and *she* ended up blushing. Now, why'd she have to do that? After all his resolves, here he was, flat on his face in love. With an engaged older woman, no less, whose ridiculous French braid was busting out in all directions.

For the next two hours they hardly stopped. Ben made the rounds from Gary to Rick to Steve and back again, piggyback or on someone's shoulders. He'd lost both shoes in mire that sucked at their feet like quicksand, in a place that had panicked Clyde as much as it had the younger two.

Even Amy took a turn with Ben on her back. "You

186

have to clean my room four Saturdays in a row for this," she said, choking from his death grip on her neck.

The water was swift and up to their chests where the canyon was narrowest. If lightweight Neale hadn't been between Rick and Gary once when she lost footing, she'd have been carried away. After that they cut ropes to use as tethers for the younger two. Audrey, as short as she was, dropped into several holes, but Steve was always there to pull her out. Privately, Clyde cited her for courage. She'd come up blubbering and gasping, her face full of terror, but always end up smiling somehow.

They heard the roar of a falls a hundred yards before they could see what the noise meant. Their faces grew grim, and Clyde knew they were all remembering that first logjam. Suddenly no one was talking.

Clyde looked at Rick, who was now taking much of Clyde's weight on his shoulder, but Rick was keeping his eyes on the canyon. The roaring grew more ominous. He could barely make it in smooth, gliding water; how would he handle turbulence? Clyde's stomach started shaking and prickles rose on his neck.

Clyde took a deep breath and sent a prayer up the cliffs. Why am I doing that? The Narrows won't listen. In answer to gravity, the Virgin River had sculpted every inch of this masterpiece. It wasn't about to let mere humans interfere.

Their way was blocked, it turned out, by a boulder the size of a living room, a massive sandstone plug that had probably been there for hundreds of years. It angled in toward the right side of the cliff, where everything loose appeared to have lodged during the flood. On the left, over smaller boulders, water crashed and sprayed halfway up the giant sloping rock. If they got through, it would mean crossing that forty-five degree slope, with as much chance of going into the churning river as not.

Steve pulled them together so they could hear each other over the roar. Ben, back in the water again, stood pressed against Amy's side, his eyes like moons. Clyde wondered if his own face was as white.

"I knew this was coming up, but I never saw it with high water," Steve shouted. "Who wants to rope up with me to try it out?"

No one volunteered until Audrey raised her hand.

"Go on, babe!" Steve lowered her hand. "You're not heavy enough."

"I will," Gary said. "What do we do?"

Steve got his rope out of the pack Amy was wearing. "I better cross first. You belay me. I'll anchor it—use my body if I have to. Gary, you wear the harness, come across last. Rick, Audrey, Amy"—

he pointed their order—"then feed the kids across. That way we have help at either end."

"One at a time or buddies?" Rick yelled. His face was pasty, too.

"One at a time. Be easier if someone falls in—"

"What if I fall in?" Ben asked with a grimace.

"Hang on to the rope. We'll have you tied with the other rope while you follow the guide rope. Think you can do it?"

Ben looked doubtful.

"Sure he can," Clyde spoke up. "He's done lots harder stuff than that."

"Before you come," Steve yelled in Gary's ear, "lash all the sticks together at the end of Ben's rope once he gets across. We'll ferry 'em over some way."

Gary nodded that he understood, then they moved into the channel again, buddies holding hands, everyone keeping to the right canyon wall.

The roar pounded their ears, making talking impossible when they got near. They crowded together on some rocks. The river sent spray up their legs as they watched Steve get ready, watched him tie one end of Clyde's rope around Neale, indicating that she'd go ahead of Ben when the time came.

Gary got into the harness, pulling it tight at his waist, then Steve whipped the same rope around himself. After another glance around, he pointed to the daypack Amy was wearing, then to himself. Did she want him to take it? She shook her head no.

Clyde could hardly breathe watching the panto-mime. He'd never been such a shaking mess in his life—stiff-legged, weak, scared. He doubled, *tripled* his promises to get his mother out of town.

Steve started high on the slope, with Gary feeding out line as he went. He kept low, barely creeping along. It looked easy enough at first and he made good time; then his left foot slipped and his hands flew out to grab at the smooth rock. He dropped to his knees, still groping. Just above the water, he caught himself, held, tensely searched for a foothold. He twisted slightly at the hips, then angled his tennis shoes and started inching back up the rock. He slipped again and again on the wet sandstone, but slowly he was clawing his way back up.

Audrey, standing stiff and scared next to Clyde, never took her eyes off Steve. Without thinking, Clyde put his arm around her, then never gave himself a breath until Steve got all the way across. At the end he scuttled sideways like a nervous black crab, then dropped off the rock and out of sight.

A second later he popped up, waved, and they knew he was safe. They all cheered with relief.

Rick crawled up to be next, his jaw set like he was going to the guillotine. The rope was the answer. He slipped, too, but he hung on, guiding himself with one hand, balancing with the other, grabbing with both only once when he fell. The rope sagged and all the color drained from his face when it happened, but he got back up, then finally across, jumping off the rock next to Steve with what looked like a whoop of joy.

Audrey went next, then Amy, with the women being more steady on the rock than the men. Even with the daypack, Amy walked right along, staying higher than the rest of them. Her confidence almost unnerved Clyde, whose turn was next.

He limped over to the rock, sat on the edge, and swung his bad leg up. He had to have Gary's hand to get to his feet. Ben patted him on the rear and Neale shouted something. Four people have done it—it can be done, he told himself, pumping up his courage.

He gripped the rope with his right hand, gripped it hard. When he straightened, he felt his knees buckling under him. The right knee killed him at that angle. Suddenly his hand, his whole arm, was shaking with fear he couldn't control. Steve had said, "Lean away from the rock," but how do you lean away when you have to lean in? And if he fell? The knee was swollen so tight, it wouldn't bend. How would he get back up?

Clyde stood there paralyzed, unable to take even one step. He wanted to back off, but that didn't work either. His chest heaved. *Go! You have to do it!* He couldn't! He'd be tumbled in the rapids, pinned to the bottom, he knew it . . . like surfing, a wave rolling him over and over . . .

"I can't!" he finally shouted into the air. "I can't do it!"

Out of the corner of his eye, he could see Gary motioning, but he couldn't turn around. His whole body had gone rigid. He just stood there hanging on, his face wet with the cold spray, the noise pounding his ears—terrified!

Then Neale was behind him, sliding her arm around his waist. She turned his head, made him see her. She was nodding for him to go on, telling him without words that she was next and he had to hurry. She hit the back of his knee with hers and forced the first step, his leg jerking in response to the pain she'd caused.

"The other one!" she yelled at his ear. He slid his other foot forward.

She didn't turn back, she stayed with him, her left hand tight on his stomach. He'd step, she'd step, her body pressing him, urging him on. It took an hour to get across, it seemed, but they came in like a tandem act and were helped down at the end of the rock onto a level slab.

Clyde felt like crying, he was so ashamed, but all the hugs and pats kept him from it. Suddenly Neale buried her head in his chest, her skinny arms around him like a vise. He thought she'd never let go. When she did, he could see she'd been crying.

"What the hell?" he said, laughing with relief. "Don't cry, Neale, I've got you!" And he hugged and rocked her until she started laughing, too.

15

By noon they were out of the most dangerous section and into the big loops, with less than two miles to go. Clyde's face was the color of chalk and he hardly talked, though Neale sometimes got a word out of him with her nonstop chatter. It now took Rick and Gary on either side to keep him on his feet.

During a rest stop at the Orderville Gulch junction, Rick had asked Steve why a climbing rescue team couldn't just haul Clyde up the cliff with ropes. "They could pick him up with a helicopter right up there on the plateau, fly him straight to a hospital." It had sounded easy enough.

"You kidding?" Clyde cried in alarm. "I'm not a basket case yet."

Steve, too, had quickly vetoed the idea. "Trying to get him 1500 feet to the top would be more dangerous than having him walk it. We're pretty close if we can all hold out."

At least the water was warmer here at midday. Every once in a while Amy could relax enough to look up and take in the cliffs, which were bathed in the orangey glow of diffused sunlight.

"You know something?" Amy said to Audrey, swinging around to see how far ahead they were. "This would be a really pleasant little hike if we weren't so hungry and beat."

"Maybe. If you also take away the stiff current, the wet clothes, my miserable, blackened toenails. Oh yes, and the mud content. I wouldn't have to drop out of sight if I could see the bottom."

Amy grinned at her. "I bet those fourth graders at school love you. I wish I'd had more teachers like you."

"I'm the one who loves them. What would I do without my kids?"

Probing through a rocky, noisy stretch of rapids, Amy wondered if she'd ever enjoy the whisperings of a gentle creek again. She herself had forgotten how to speak in anything but a shout, but conversation with a buddy made things easier and she wasn't about to give it up.

"Let's trade addresses when we get out," Audrey shouted now. "We can send survivor cards back and forth every Labor Day."

Amy nodded big, called out, "Okay by me."

"Steve and I also want to give you a wedding gift. I hope that's all right. After all we've been through together—"

The wedding! Amy's cheeks grew hot. What was she going to do? All those gifts piling up at home, Debbi shopping for a new dress, the plans she'd made with the florist, who also happened to be her mother's best friend . . .

"Oh Audrey," she blurted out, "there may not be a wedding." She blinked and swallowed, trying not to break down.

They walked on, holding tight to each other's hands. Amy could feel herself trembling. She knew what was going on in Audrey's mind: Is this the time or place to decide? Her mother would say the same thing.

As the canyon widened, they came into shallower, calmer water where it was easier to talk, where Amy *could* talk, having found some control.

"Strange how things are," Audrey said finally, tucking Amy's hand in against her side for a minute. "Here I've been envying you and Rick. I guess a person should never envy someone else's happiness."

"You've been envying us?" It was Amy's turn to be startled. "This whole time I've been thinking, I want a marriage like Audrey's. I want to feel the way you two do about each other. It's obvious you're crazy about—I mean, you guys really love each other. Gary, too, with Debbi. It's just that—what am I trying to say?"

She took a breath, searched for words. "I can't marry Rick simply out of the habit of being with him . . . and because we turn each other on. I want more than that. Am I making any sense? Or does this all sound kind of, you know . . . hysterical?"

"You're making big sense." Audrey said, but with a funny expression.

A minute later, using their poles to probe over a submerged log, Audrey said, "Look, Amy, Steve and I aren't married. I guess I'm still old-fashioned enough to be embarrassed about vacationing together, but we honestly weren't trying to deceive anyone. It was just easier to go along . . . let you people assume . . ."

"But you're wearing rings!" Amy noticed everyone's rings these days. Audrey wore a wedding set; Steve didn't.

"Oh, I'm married all right. My husband, Frank, is in a nursing home in Salt Lake. He has Huntington's chorea, a very sad, impossible disease. It ends disastrously, if you know anything about it."

"Oh dear! I'm so sorry, Audrey. My problems are nothing—"

"No, no, you mustn't say that. Everyone's problems are valid. Really!"

"Isn't there any hope for him?"

197

"No, and it's been eight years. He doesn't know me and we don't have any kind of life together. But Amy—" Suddenly she was the one near tears. "I came on this trip with Steve planning to tell him I'd move to Seattle so we could at least be together."

Amy held her breath. "And now you're not?"

"What has this place done to all of us?" Audrey cried, and Amy could feel her pain welling up. "There I was, facing death and thinking about what would happen to my parakeet! Do you see what I'm saying? If I walk away, there's no one to worry about Frank. As poor as my devotion is, it's better than nothing. I go in, and I hold his hand and I talk. Sometimes I go home and cry. But I'm all he has."

Amy didn't have any idea what to say. How could Audrey be so cheerful, so caring about everyone else with such a load on her mind?

Then, characteristically, Audrey pulled Amy to a stop and turned to check on the others, who were now out of sight around a bend. She wrinkled up her pixie nose as she swung back to say, "We were really striding out."

"Think we ought to wait?" asked Amy. It made her nervous not being able to see Ben. "Maybe you and I should spell the guys and help Clyde."

They spotted a huge fin of rock that ran down the cliff like a giant tree root—a place where they could be out of the current—so they headed for that.

"Given a chance to talk," Audrey admitted in a wry voice, "I could cross the finish line and not know it."

They scooted their rear ends up against the cliff and braced their feet on another rock above water. Stretching the sore muscles of her legs and resting her back felt awfully good to Amy.

"Sorry I dumped on you," Audrey said as they twisted their sticks into the mud between them. "But your wedding, Amy, such a heartbreaker! This trip has been tough on both you kids. Men seem to feel solely responsible in dangerous situations, and they really shouldn't, you know? They aren't made of steel any more than we are."

Amy nodded and stared down at the black water. "It isn't that I don't love Rick. I do. I really care what happens to him."

"Yes, and it shows. But loving someone doesn't necessarily mean sharing a life in marriage. I know that firsthand."

Amy sighed. She looked up to see dozens of stone fly exoskeletons still fastened to the rock . . . because they happened to be protected in a fissure. She could identify. It was as if her heart or some vital part of her had disappeared, leaving behind a hollow shell looking exactly like Amy Lloyd.

"I'm not sure Rick and I see the world the same way," she said to Audrey now, still trying to explain her own mind. "Or value the same things. Is that what it is? Sometimes it's like—well—like we're standing in two different places, and too often back to back.

"Could be I'm not ready," Amy continued. "No, I think I've known it from the beginning, but it was losing Ben for a while . . . that's what did it! I don't have those kinds of family feelings for Rick, and I think I should have if we're going to marry."

Audrey nodded, her face full of concern, and Amy thought of her mother.

"Oh help!" She suddenly rolled her eyes. "Can you see my mother when I tell her? With everything in motion . . . a hundred guests?"

Audrey laughed. "She'll be so thrilled to see you walk in that door you could tell her anything."

"I'll remember that. Hey, Mom, guess what? I changed my mind. We can still run an ad, can't we? 'Wedding dress, size 8 . . . never worn.' "

Then it didn't seem so funny, and Amy had a hard time dealing with the boulder-size lump in her throat.

"Maybe—" Audrey said after a silence, "maybe a crisis makes us look extra hard at how much risk we're willing to take. We only have so many hours, so many days in this life, and every decision affects what comes after. Occasionally we're able to take the long view or one that makes a difference. I don't know. . . ." She patted Amy's hand. "Good luck to us both! Anyway, thanks for listening."

"I sure wish things were different for you and Steve," Amy replied. "He's so neat. Will he wait?"

Audrey inspected her dirty nails, thought a minute, then looked up and smiled. "Yes, I honestly think he will."

"He's crazy if he doesn't," Amy said back.

When they finally came to a skinny riverbank, Clyde asked for another stop. The place was strewn with bread-loaf rocks, but it was still a bank.

While the others tossed rocks to make a place for Clyde to lie down, Amy dug out her sleeping bag and spread it on the gravel. Then she and Gary eased Clyde to the ground. Audrey brought over the water bottle and made him take some more Tylenol.

No one knew what to do with the terrible-looking leg, but Neale decided it should be elevated, so she got busy and made a ramp of smooth rocks rising from his hip to ten inches or so. Carefully, she placed his right leg on it, her folded windbreaker under the knee.

"Thanks," Clyde said and closed his eyes. "That helps." He was white to the lips. Amy suspected he was nauseated with pain.

Ben was in amazingly good spirits, having been toted all the way, but Amy made him take a Tylenol, too. His feet were huge, filling the muddy, blood-spotted socks to capacity. Steve dropped him down next to Clyde, where he stayed. In fact, after Clyde raised up and patted himself on the stomach, Ben had a place to rest his head.

"What are friends for?" Ben mumbled, crawling over, then sprawling on his back over rocks and everything. "I know," he told Clyde, "you like being my pillow better than anything else."

Clyde grinned weakly. "You got it, bro."

Already they've adopted each other, Amy thought, dropping down on a rock herself.

Although driftwood was scattered up and down the bank, no one, not even Steve the pyromaniac, had the energy to make a fire at first. They all just sat there, shivering in their wet clothes. There was talk of Gary and Rick going out ahead to send back help with a Stokes litter or to get a doctor, but so far no one moved.

Finally it was Neale who jumped up, hyper as ever, and charged around gathering up anything small, dry, or burnable. She set a match to it and got a fire going—of which she was very proud. Expansively she invited everyone over, *insisted* they all move over to the fire to warm themselves.

"Oh my gosh," Rick said, once he was on his feet, "look what's coming!"

The others stood. Eight or ten people, three in Park Service uniforms, were working their way upstream with hiking sticks. About half of them were wearing packs.

"Has to be a search party," Steve said. "The Narrows would be closed to the public after that kind of flood." Soon they were waving back and forth, and Rick made a scrambling effort to tuck in his shirt.

Audrey, of all people, burst into tears and had to cover her face.

Steve reached for her. "Now she cries, my tough one!" Awkwardly, he patted her head, wiped her cheeks. "Can't stand good news, huh?"

Amy knew why she was crying, and it wasn't only relief. In a matter of hours, Steve was supposed to be on a plane headed back to Seattle.

It was all excited talk and confusion as the rangers and Iron County Search-and-Rescue arrived, looked over the situation, asked questions, took down their names, then went about preparing their portable litter for Clyde. They made a second litter for Ben out of Amy's sleeping bag and two sticks.

A ranger got on a hand radio, explaining that he probably couldn't get a response here in the Narrows, but sometimes it happened. "KOJ770," he said several times before putting the radio back in its holster. "I'll keep trying. I think a life-flight helicopter out of Vegas might be the fastest."

On her other side, Amy heard someone telling

Neale that a party of ten got out yesterday after the rain. "I haven't talked to them myself, but they had some close calls. Legs and ankles hammered pretty bad."

Neale came away with her eyes shining, her lips pressed tight. The look she and Clyde exchanged after she bent to tell him had understanding written all over it.

"Friends of yours," they told Gary, "spent the night at the lodge. The two of them have been waiting around all day."

"—with your wife and baby," the woman ranger added with a quick smile.

Gary yelled, "Yahoo!" and a couple rescuers clapped him on the back.

Amy couldn't believe how happy the rangers were acting. Some of the rescue party even had tears in their eyes when they came up out of the water.

"You were presumed dead," Chris, the woman ranger, told them. "Three inches of rain fell on Cedar Mountain Saturday night, which is unheard of! Nationwide TV stuff here . . . the whole country's been praying for you." She took off her hat, tucked in some blond hairs, then set the Park Service hat straight across her head again. Lowering her pack next, she asked if anyone was hungry or thirsty.

Her question brought Ben straight to his feet shouting, "What d'ya got?"

The rest of them weren't much more mannerly,

behaving exactly like a pack of drooling dogs. They all crowded around, watching intently as she slipped string off a shoe box.

"Jesus!" Rick said with awe when she took off the lid. "Chocolate chip cookies."

Chris grinned. "Home baked yesterday after the rain turned us around. We didn't get this far when we had to turn back." She handed the box to Ben—smiling and nodding. "Just help yourselves. Please!"

They *fell* on the cookies—even Audrey. Rick, before putting a single bite in his own mouth, scooped up a handful and gave them to Clyde. Chris, still breathing hard from the hike, brought out a thermos next and poured coffee into foam cups. She then stood by and watched—happily, Amy thought, suspecting that what they were eating was the rangers' lunch.

The feast of coffee and cookies was so wonderful Amy had to squeeze her eyes tight to keep back the tears. She'd never tasted anything so good! She never would again, either—she knew. Afterward, closing the empty box, the eight of them couldn't thank Chris enough.

Finally, with Clyde lying ashen-faced on one litter and Ben smiling regally from the other, their expanded party of seventeen walked back into the Virgin River for what Amy hoped would be her last hike in the Narrows.

It had been a long journey, and Amy had no idea

how she'd made it. Her legs were quivering, her ankles shot; she was bruised, dirty, smelly, cold, and exhausted. She felt even worse inside, knowing this might also be her last hike with Rick. She gripped his hand, hoping they could somehow still be friends, but knowing a casual relationship mightn't be possible anymore.

Amy sighed for the hundredth time. Having been raised in a family where breaking a promise was more than a misdemeanor, she didn't know how in the world she was going to explain herself to anyone.

"Less than an hour," one of the rescue party called out, "and you folks will be home free."

Rick gave her a squeeze.

Home free? Not quite.

From the final bend they could see the crowd that had gathered up ahead. A radio message had apparently gotten to the dispatcher. The river, less than knee deep now and fifty feet wide, broadened to become the mouth of the Zion Narrows. There were cameras and newspeople everywhere. Some of them were wading right into the water to meet them.

Amy felt silly trying to straighten her clothes, but she did anyway, then shrugged and resigned herself. There was no way to improve anything.

"I asked those reporters to keep out of the river,"

one ranger shouted to another. "You can see what good it did!"

A reporter collared Amy when she came abreast and offered her a hand, but she stepped around him. "I'm used to it," she said. "I'm okay."

"Can you tell me what happened to you folks in there? Where were you when it hit?" *He* wasn't doing so well, sliding all over the place as he tried to stay alongside.

Rick, who'd dropped her hand, was already surrounded by journalists and talking up a storm.

The man with Amy said, "Anybody in your party missing? Must have been rough going in there, the way you all look."

"Gee, thanks," Amy answered with a grin. "Say, why don't you talk to him?" She pointed back at Rick. "I'm too dead, honest!"

She turned the other way to see what had happened to Audrey, who'd been just behind her until now. She and Steve had fallen back and were walking with their arms around each other. She saw them stop, kiss, then Audrey moved out ahead of Steve, her face a disaster, and came on alone.

Acting purely on intuition, Amy stopped to wait, her back still to the reporter. Impatient apparently, he shouldered his camera and struck out after Gary.

Audrey linked arms with Amy as soon as she caught up.

"There are thirty-one fourth graders depending on me," she said in a stricken voice. "I'm a school-teacher and I have a job to do. Keep reminding me, will you?"

"Oh Audrey," Amy burst out, "it's not fair!"

"Would the press believe us if we told them that? I don't think so. We're supposed to be jubilant."

Finally, close enough to the paved trail to see individuals, Amy's eyes darted over the crowd trying to spot Debbi and little Jessica.

She saw another news crew and some hot-food containers, plus dozens of tourist types, half of them snapping pictures. To think she'd be immortalized stringy-haired in someone's photo album, wearing clothes she planned to burn!

As they walked out of the river and up the left bank, someone was there putting blankets over their backs, thrusting hot drinks at them.

It was a loud, happy, emotional welcome, with the crackling of hand radios—"Missing hikers, all eight, now at the mouth"—adding excitement.

Still searching for a familiar face, Amy found one. Her dad's. His mouth was working as he made his way through the crowd, trying to cover his feelings but not succeeding. They both broke into tears well before they reached each other. Her mother was right behind him, and seconds later Ben was in their arms, too, as his makeshift sleeping-bag stretcher came alongside.

Amy could hear Rick's parents, too, and she looked for them next. When Mrs. Chidester found Amy, she wailed, "We thought we'd lost our son *and* our daughter-in-law!" They hugged a long time. Amy dearly loved Rick's mother.

She was still surrounded when Neale pushed past screaming, "Mom, Mom!" and she saw the two of them fall on each other's necks, crying with identical loud gulps. Amy had never seen such a reunion as Neale and her mother were having!

The rangers were busy handing up Clyde's litter when Amy realized she mightn't see him again if she didn't get over there right away. She asked her folks to wait, then threaded through the crowd of people to where fresh help from the rescue unit were taking over.

She saw Clyde's hand in the air trying for someone's attention, heard him call, "Where's Amy?" When she got to him he was up on his elbows, making a fuss. "We can't go yet," he insisted.

"I'm right here," she cried, rushing up and grabbing his hand. "Oh, Clyde, you're going to be okay, I know you are—my first real-life hero, I'll never forget you."

Suddenly Neale was there, too, taking his hand on the other side, as the litter bearers lifted him for the hike out over the paved trail.

"Good-bye," Neale cried, "good-bye, dear Clyde. I don't think you're a klutz at all. You're going to get the longest letter from me in the hospital!"

"My gosh, your address," Amy shouted. "Neale, help me remember it."

Clyde lifted Amy's hand, shook it fiercely. "If she can remember the dumb lyrics to all those ballads, she can remember my address."

"Shoot!" Neale said. "I'll memorize it."

He made Neale repeat it twice, then asked them to tell everyone else good-bye. "And Ben—" He closed his eyes, as if everything was too much effort. "Tell him I'll be fine."

"What's wrong with him?" A well-built kid with sun streaks in his hair rushed up from the other direction. He put a hand on the stretcher and trotted along in front of Amy.

Clyde lifted his head, said, "Heeeeeey, Jake—" then fell back again.

"Jason!" Amy and Neale exclaimed at the same time.

The guy looked surprised to hear his name, but quickly turned back to Clyde.

"You won't believe any of it," Clyde said feebly, "but it's all true."

Neale and Amy let them go on, Clyde and his best friend, Jason, who looked almost too immaculate in his white tennies and shorts.

When Amy remembered Audrey again, she was nowhere to be seen. Steve either. Amy bit her lip.

They'd slipped away without addresses. She couldn't even remember their funny last names!

Back with her folks, who were quizzing Ben, she learned that they and the Chidesters had rented a plane to search the canyon, but without luck.

"All that money," her mother said, "and we couldn't see beans!"

"You were in that plane?" Ben's mouth fell open as he swayed along on a litter between their dad, Chris, and two others. "I knew it! I knew that was somebody after me, I could just tell."

Amy looked around until she saw Rick and then waited for him. They took hands. His eyes were incredibly sad, and she wondered if he already knew. She hoped he hadn't heard anything from Gary.

"You want to come back someday?" he asked as they walked slowly after the others. "Maybe we could find the stuff we lost."

"No thanks," she said. What they'd lost was lost.

"Listen," he told her, "Dad's buying the steaks tonight. He wants all of you to meet us in St. George— Gary and Debbi, Neale and her folks, too."

"We'll probably go to the emergency room with Ben first," Amy said. "But maybe then—sounds good to me. I can't see past a hot bath and a bed right now, can you?"

A National Wildlife photographer approached them wanting pictures and an interview, but Amy begged off. "You go ahead," she told Rick, who seemed willing enough. "I want to stay with Ben."

The place was swarming with people the rest of the way to the parking lot, but Amy mostly noticed the sun coming through the trees, how it dappled arms, faces, the rocks, the trail. What incredible strength she was taking home from the Narrows! How could a person be so exhausted and feel so strong at the same time?

Looking ahead for her folks and Ben, Amy saw a little kid—a boy who might have been in the fourth grade—coming toward her with great purpose, darting in and around other people as he called her name. When she got his attention, he stopped and pulled a piece of paper out of his pocket.

"It's from somebody up there," he pointed vaguely. Then he pinned her with a look. "You sure you're Amy?"

She nodded, grinned. "Positive!"

It was an address and phone number with Audrey Heins' name at the top. Bottom right—incredibly— was a smiley face that looked just like her.